To Louise
wishes.

Roger Sayers

CW01574737

PAWS

A catalogue record of this book is available from the British Library

First Edition: May 2003

ISBN: 1-84375-021-X

To order additional copies of this book please visit:
http://www.upso.co.uk/rogersayers.htm

Published by: UPSO Ltd
5 Stirling Road, Castleham Business Park,
St Leonards-on-Sea, East Sussex TN38 9NW United Kingdom
Tel: 01424 853349 Fax: 01424 854084
Email: info@upso.co.uk Web: http://www.upso.co.uk

PAWS

by

Roger Sayers

UPSO

Chapter 1

Off-duty Police Sergeant Harry Stoke felt self conscious in his borrowed flying suit. Jenny Wells wore one too, but she was a pilot and the yellow overall suited her. Jenny handed him a helmet, coloured yellow like their flying clothing, and told him to try it for size. The fit was not bad. Jenny helped him with the unfamiliar fastenings of his goggles.

'Keep them on all the time we're flying,' she instructed him, 'there may not be any insects today but never take risks. You don't want a bug in your eye at fifty knots, or a bird. Take them off now and I'll show you where we're going.'

Stoke did as he was told.

'Does that happen often?' he enquired with just a hint of anxiety.

'Hardly ever,' Jenny replied, 'but I've seen what happens when it does and it isn't funny. I'm going to have a bird strike today, thirty seconds after we take off.'

'What do you mean?' Stoke blurted, 'How do you know?'

Jenny Wells smiled but she wasn't laughing.

'I don't, and I'm not prepared to take chances either.'

Jenny Wells had an air of competence and professionalism. Harry Stoke felt reassured. Spreading her maps on the table she traced a path with her fingertip. One map was an aeronautical chart with markings that were unfamiliar to Stoke and he asked for an explanation. He pointed to one of the symbols.

'Spot height, the same as on the ordnance survey map except the figures in red next to it is the height above mean sea level,' Jenny explained, and showed him another, 'you see how the red figures are always the larger figure?'

Stoke showed his understanding. Jenny indicated some other markings.

'This is an airways route, this section runs between Exeter and Cardiff International Airport. It's ten miles wide, nautical miles that is, and it's a sort of main road for commercial air traffic. It won't affect us because we'll be below its lower height limit and I don't intend to fly under it anyway.'

'How far is ten nautical miles in real miles?' Stoke asked.

Jenny spun the face of her dead reckoning computer and showed him the arrows marked 'Naut' and 'Stat.'

'Eleven and a half statute miles as near as makes any difference,' she said.

'That's close enough for me,' Stoke replied.

'It'll do. Now look at this place, this is important, it's a military air traffic zone. They won't bother us if we don't bother them but they operate helicopters on the moors sometimes and they fly fast and low. Sing out if you see one, or any other aircraft. I might have seen it already but I might not, so don't make any assumptions, OK?'

'OK, but what if you have the right of way?'

'Famous last words, but I don't intend them to be mine. I'm serious Harry. If we meet anything I'll make a steep turn and show as much of my wing as I can. It would be interesting to phone them afterwards and see if it worked.'

Harry Stoke looked at her to see if she was joking. He thought not.

Pilot and passenger walked out to Jenny's aircraft. Harry had wondered why a yellow machine was called the Red Arrow.

'It's yellow because yellow is usually the easiest colour to see, and it got its name because I'm a fan of the Red Arrows aerobatic team.'

As she helped him with the seat straps Harry Stoke felt that Jenny's explanation had a certain obscure logic.

Looking down on the moors from two thousand feet Harry Stoke began to really enjoy his first experience of flying in microlight aircraft, and dimly perceived Jenny's enthusiasm for flying. She had casually mentioned the use of the blue bag tucked into the pocket above his left knee, then told him to forget it. He wondered if she carried one too. It seemed likely; Jenny Wells was obviously not the kind of pilot who left anything to chance.

A sharp bend in the A396 road was one of Jenny's turning points. Stoke watched as it came up underneath them and then the aircraft banked in a smooth turn and he tried to remember what he had been told about the wind. Something about feeling it in your face, and if it blew from the side your flying was sloppy and you were losing height.

Jennifer Well's turn was perfect.

Half an hour later Jenny flew a wide circle round her home, and Stoke knew she was checking up on her father's sheep at their small farm, and then she touched down smoothly on the field that her father permitted her to fly from and switched off her engine outside the barn where she kept her aircraft.

'I kept my eyes open but I didn't see any other aircraft,' Harry said as he removed his helmet.

'You missed two, but don't worry, it's not always easy, and we'll never know how many I missed, will we? And I must phone Mr North, one of his troughs has dried up again and his poor cows were all standing round it for a drink of water.' Jenny smiled. 'Local knowledge, isn't that what you call it in the police?'

Neither had seen the lonely figure far below them, uselessly tracking their flight with his single barrelled shotgun, and if the lone poacher had seen what was watching him, he would have fled.

Chapter 2

Ronnie Gleaves stood watching the television set in the corner of the room while he waited for the weather forecaster to finish his summary.

'The mild weather will give way to more unsettled conditions as the front moves eastwards through the night. There may be isolated thunderstorms,' he pointed vaguely at the chart and continued. 'Winds will be light to moderate. That's all from me, I'll be back tomorrow.'

Gleaves sniffed audibly and wiped his nose on a well-used tissue that he stuffed back in his pocket.

'I'm going out now Dad,' he said.

His father shrugged his shoulders and put a half empty beer can on the floor beside his chair.

'You'll get caught again one of these times,' he said without turning round. His eyes never left the television screen. Ronnie Gleaves sniffed again.

'No chance, not again. Here, did I tell you what one of the boys saw?' Without waiting for an answer he continued, 'He saw a big animal up on the hill, a deer he reckons. I might get a shot at it. That'd be all right wouldn't it? I've never had a deer before.'

The man slumped deeper into his armchair and made no reply except to shrug his shoulders again. He reached for the beer can. Ronnie Gleaves sniffed and left the room.

Outside the house he studied the sky, then crossed the yard where his father ran a bit of a business repairing farm machinery, and climbed into an old Bedford van that had seen better days. The engine started at the third attempt and a dog barked at the sound. The barking came from inside the workshop on the far side of the yard. Gleaves gave a smirk of satisfaction. Going to be a good dog that was, he thought, when he'd trained it, like. Only cost him a few quid too, pretty good for an Alsatian bitch. He would think up a good name for it, something classy. How about Sheba? That sounded good. He spoke the name out loud.

'Sheba.'

Sounded real great.

The battered van rattled down a country lane. Gleaves whistled tunelessly and sniffed occasionally. He drove into a rutted track, half hidden by low-branched oaks, and switched the engine off.

Donning a dirty jacket, he took a length of light wire from beneath the passenger seat, and then he filled his pockets with shotgun cartridges. Finally, reaching behind him, he pulled a single barrelled shotgun from beneath a piece of sacking. He was ready for a spot of poaching.

Ronnie Gleaves was twenty-seven years old, beanpole thin, with sharp features. His habit of giving a short sniff every few minutes had earned him the nickname 'Sniffer.' He was a petty thief, not very successfully, and a poacher, which was his favourite occupation. He was a very good shot with his twelve-bore gun.

About ninety minutes of daylight remained as Sniffer set out for the woods. It was an uphill walk of about half a mile, and he stayed close to the hedges as he walked. A light breeze stirred the fresh young leaves.

Sniffer Gleaves studied the weather again and reckoned it would hold.

He plodded uphill, glancing frequently over his shoulder to see if he was observed. When he reached the wood he walked along the fenced edge, studying the ground until he found what he was looking for, a rabbit run where the grass was flattened as the animals passed along their regular trail. There was another run close by, and fresh droppings. That was good.

Gleaves laid his gun down and carefully fashioned a snare with the wire he had brought with him. The deadly noose hung a hand's-breadth above the ground.

That ought to do nicely, he thought. Picking up the gun he loaded a cartridge into the breech. Carefully and quietly he slipped under the fence. He hoped to shoot a roosting pheasant or two, and maybe he would get a shot at that deer!

Forty minutes later Sniffer was frustrated and angry. There hadn't been any rabbits, nor any pheasants. That was funny, now he came to think about it. There were no birds around at all. And what about the rabbits? He hadn't seen a single thing. Might as well pack it in, he thought, but I'll just have a look at my snares and see if I've had any luck there. Should make it before it got too dark to see anything.

Holding his gun in his right hand while he gripped a fence post with his left, Sniffer put one foot on the lower strand of barbed wire and pulled himself up. He swung his leg over the fence and his foot tipped the top wire and he lost his balance and jerked the trigger convulsively. A blast of shot tore through the undergrowth.

The scream of agony that ripped through the night made Sniffer's hair stand on end. Stunned, he fell off the fence. A second scream hit him like a blow and the poacher saw an animal writhing on the ground inches from where he lay. It looked huge in the fast fading light. The animal rolled over in agony and waved a shattered and bloody paw in the air. Seeing Ronnie Gleaves cowering with fear it struggled to stand on only three legs.

Sniffer felt the beast's breath on his face as the thing stood over him, and screwed his eyes shut and drew in his arms and legs in a pathetic attempt to make himself small. Slitted pupils glared down at him as if the animal wanted to remember his face, then with another shrill cry of pain it backed away slowly. Then it was gone.

Whimpering with fear, Gleaves scrambled to his feet and fled, faster than he had ever run in his life, not stopping until he was back in his van with the door locked. Many minutes passed before his shaking hand was able to turn the ignition key.

***

Police Constable David Windsley pedalled briskly along the road in a cheerful mood on his way to work.

Passing a road sign he read it out loud, 'Mud on road,' and added, 'work, three hundred yards.'

Once he had managed to wake up and get out of bed - not necessarily in that order, he often joked - Windsley enjoyed the early shift, working from six in the morning until two in the afternoon. After four years in the force he had managed to get used to early rising but the first few minutes were always hard.

A rural beat officer, he worked from a small station on the edge of the moors. He steered his cycle off the road and freewheeled up the path, tapping a window as he cycled to the rear of the building.

Inside, PC Al Croft spoke first.

'Morning Windy, I had the kettle on before I heard your knock on the window. I'll brew up, I fancy a cup before I go off duty. One sugar?'

David Windsley unbuttoned his jacket.

'Please. Quiet night?'

Croft smothered a yawn.

'Fairly quiet. The usual Sunday night stuff around closing time but nothing to get worked up about.'

Picking up the telephone Windsley said, 'I'll ring in while you're brewing up and I'll ring you off at the same time. Is there anything you want me to say?'

'Tell them I want a pay rise and no more night shifts. I'll get the coffee on the go.'

Windsley made his call to headquarters.

'PC Croft?' A voice asked.

'No. I'll fetch him if you like. This is PC Windsley.'

'Oh, morning Dave, I didn't recognise you. Have you got a lot on this morning?'

'Not so far,' Windsley replied. 'There are a couple of summonses left over from last week and I'll try to catch them before they go to work, if they do, and I want to get in to the hospital later to take an accident statement. That's if they let me see him, it's from that lorry smash a couple of days ago and the driver was knocked about a bit.'

'OK, let me know if you go off your patch. Actually Dave, I wanted to talk to you, I was going to ring you later. I've a message for you to ring Sergeant Stoke at nine o'clock. He's got to see someone on your patch and he says he'll double up in your car.'

PC Windsley made a note.

'Right, ring at nine. Anything else?'

'Not yet. Drop by when you pick up Stokey and if anything comes up I'll hold it till you get here, right?'

'Will do.'

PC Croft placed a cup in front of him.

'I've used up all the milk,' he informed Windsley, 'there's fifty pence in the kitty.'

Then he was gone.

David Windsley leafed through a few papers, reports to be handed in when he called in at headquarters later in the morning. He worked carefully and methodically and by the time he finished it was almost seven o'clock. Adding the last file to the others in the out tray, he stood up and stretched.

He checked the oil and water and inspected the tyres of his vehicle and sat with the engine running while he made a test transmission on the radio. This done, he drove off.

Three young cyclists with newspaper delivery bags slung over their shoulders moved from three abreast to single file when they saw his car. Leaving the main highway he drove uphill on a narrow road, and spotting a milk float approaching he remembered the milk money he had left in the office kitty. Never mind, he could pay out of his own pocket and make it up later, so he flashed his headlights to the driver and pulled over, while the float halted fifty yards away on the opposite side of the road. The driver seemed excited about something as he walked towards the waiting policeman.

Windsley called out, 'Morning Dan. Can you spare a pint?'

'Hello Mr Windsley. I'm glad I met you, it's saved me a trip to your station. I've got a bit of news for you.'

'Good news or bad?'

Replying in short sentences, Dan Horrocks removed his cap and scratched his bald scalp.

'Well, I dunno really. About a mile back it was. An animal. Limping like. Just off the road, I could see it over the hedge. 'Course I didn't get much of a look. Keep my eyes on the road I do, when I'm driving. Anyway I did see it though. Know what it was?'

'Surprise me Dan.'

'I'll surprise you all right Mr Windsley. I thought it was a dog at first, a big dog. But it wasn't, it was something else. I know what it was though.'

Dan Horrocks looked expectantly at the constable.

'I thought you were telling me what it was Dan, but I'll play. What was it?'

'Yeah, well. I'll tell you,' Horrocks said, replacing his cap. 'I'll tell you all right. It was a cat I saw, a bloody great cat. You know, the one what's been seen before. That's what I saw Mr Windsley, I saw the Beast of Exmoor.'

PC Windsley laughed out loud.

'Come on Dan, I've heard you say you don't believe in that thing. And I'm damn sure I don't.'

The milkman ran his hand over his beard stubble and said slowly, 'Well Mr Windsley I'll tell you. I didn't till this morning but I do now, bloody right I do. I saw it limping along and I reckon as maybe a car might've given it a swipe or something. I didn't like the look of it, I can tell you.'

'OK Dan, I'll take a look if you like. Where was it?'

Dan Horrocks pointed back along the road while PC Windsley listened to his description of the location.

'Right Dan, I've got it. I'll look around a bit; I'm going that way anyhow, so I'll be there in about five minutes. Does that suit you?'

The man looked relieved.

'Aye, I'd be glad if you would,' he said, 'but watch how you go. I was scared, I don't mind telling you. The way it looked at me like. You know. Don't forget your milk.'

Constable Windsley thought about what the milk roundsman had told him. It was strange how every now and again somebody reported a large cat in the area, but he had no faith in the reports himself. It was obviously a mistake.

He stopped the car at the place where old Dan said he had seen the cat and got out for a look round. There was nothing to see of course.

He would have been less happy if he had known he was being watched.

The throbbing was almost unbearable but the animal made no sound as it crouched on its belly and licked its forepaw, never taking its unblinking stare from the constable. The dappled shades of early morning played on its dark flanks and camouflaged it perfectly in patterns of shifting light. Only the eyes were visible, green and implacably hostile.

***

At ten minutes to nine PC Windsley parked behind a second vehicle outside the station. Carrying his bottle of milk he entered the office and found Sergeant Stoke waiting for him.

'Morning Sergeant,' he said, 'I thought that was your car outside. I was going to give you a buzz in a minute, HQ told me you wanted a ride in the rural car.'

'Morning Windy,' Stoke replied. 'I want to see one or two people on your bit of ground so you can drive me round, and here's another summons for you to serve. Mister Ronald Brian Gleaves, alias Sniffer, bald tyre on motor vehicle. That ought to earn young Sniffer enough points to get him disqualified this time round. If it does, keep your eyes open for the stupid little pillock. He doesn't know how to stay out of trouble.'

Windsley nodded.

'OK. I'm going into town later to take a statement at the hospital,' he said.

'Wrong. Your man's not giving statements any more, he died in the night. The hospital rang HQ just before I left. Where's your accident file?'

PC Windsley handed over a file from the tray on the desk and the sergeant sat down to read it.

'I'm going to make a brew and make my pocketbook up. Want a cup?' Windsley asked.

'Thanks, I will. Don't put sugar in, I'm cutting down.'

Stoke started to read the file. Windsley placed a cup in front of him and took out his pocketbook and began to make his entries for the morning. Hesitating, he decided that a brief comment would suffice for the milk roundsman's report.

'07.45. Mr D HORROCKS, milk roundsman, reports seeing large cat-like animal. May be injured.'

Surnames were always entered in capitals. There, he thought, that should cover it.

Knowing the sergeant would want to see it, he placed the pocketbook on the desk. Ten minutes and a few brief comments later Sergeant Stoke returned the accident file to the tray.

'Now then Windy,' he said as he reached across the desk, 'let's have a look at your book.'

He scanned the pages and stopped at the entry for 07.45.

'So old Dan thinks he saw the beast then?'

'Saw something,' Windsley replied, 'but not what he thinks. Silly old bugger.'

'You don't believe him?'

'Not likely I don't. Would you?'

Stoke was slow to reply.

'Put it this way,' he said eventually, 'I've been in the force for ten years and in that time I've seen a lot of funny things. I've been called out to beat the moor for it after a sheep was chewed up. Didn't find anything of course, and to my way of thinking that was just as well. But don't forget I used to work this patch myself.'

Constable Windsley stared incredulously at the sergeant.

'Are you telling me you believe in it?' he enquired.

Stoke nodded.

'I believe in something, though I don't know what. But I do know there's something out there,' he waved his hand towards the window, 'and you'd better believe it too.'

'But a damn great cat for Pete's sake. Have you seen it yourself?'

There was another long pause before Stoke replied.

'Maybe,' he said, and changed the subject.

'Let's get back on the job, shall we? Are you ready?'

Windsley picked up his pocketbook.

'I was going to ring HQ first. I said I'd drop in when I picked you up, I didn't know you were driving out. They might have something for me.'

The sergeant growled, 'That summons was it. Pick it up and let's get moving.'

They drove in silence. Sergeant Stoke seemed lost in thought and not in the mood for conversation. Windsley soon gave up trying.

Stoke's business took some time and it was nearly one o'clock before he finally said, 'Right, let's go to the Gleaves' residence. Know where he lives?'

'I should think the car could find its own way by now,' Windsley said shortly.

He was getting a bit fed up with the sergeant's long silences.

A few miserable looking chickens squawked indignantly and fluttered out of the way when the police vehicle pulled up in Gleaves' yard.

Someone was working in the building at the side of the yard. They heard hammering and the sound of something being dropped. Suddenly a string of oaths was delivered in an angry tone. To the listening policemen it seemed that Ronnie Gleaves, aka Sniffer, was on the receiving end of a furious tirade from his father for tipping away a bath of dirty petrol, used for washing small machine parts, into a drain inside the workshop.

When the outburst was over they entered through a side door and found Gleaves senior bent over an untidy bench, hammering at a rusted bolt in a piece of metal which he had clamped in a vice. He scowled when he saw who his visitors were and returned to his work, deliberately ignoring them. Picking up a length of metal tube, Stoke crashed it down on the bench. Gleaves jerked up.

''Ere, what do you think you're doing?' he whined.

'Serving your Ronnie with a summons,' was the sharp reply, 'and I don't like being ignored when I want to talk to someone. Where is he?'

The man shuffled his feet.

'Why should I tell you?'

'Because I'm asking you and I know he was here a minute ago. And because one way or another I will serve the summons and you know it, so start using your head and tell me where he is.'

The reply was sullen.

'In the yard, he's having a smoke out there 'cause he can't light up in here, 'specially now he's gone and tipped the petrol bath down the drain. There, satisfied?'

'Thanks for your co-operation.'

The sarcasm was wasted.

A loud sniff told the policemen that Ronnie Gleaves was present and they turned to face him. He stood in the doorway, holding a length of rope that he was using as a dog lead.

Stoke looked at the dog, then clicked his fingers and said, 'Here, Sheba.'

The dog wagged its tail. Ronnie Gleaves jerked the rope viciously and the sergeant's eyes narrowed.

'I don't think I'd do that again if I were you Mr Gleaves,' he said mildly.

Ronnie Gleaves recognised two danger signs, the use of the word mister and the quiet tone of voice. He reddened and shuffled nervously. He had crossed Stoke before and knew what he could be like.

'What do you want?' he asked suspiciously.

PC Windsley answered.

'I've got a summons for you Sniffer. Come and get it.'

'What's it for?'

'Bald tyre. You expecting something else then?'

'Nah.'

'I also have to ascertain your plea,' Windsley continued.

'What?'

'Guilty or not guilty.'

A crafty smile spread across Gleaves' face.

'Oh, that. Not guilty. 'Course.'

'Reckon you'll get off then?' Stoke asked him.

'Nah. No chance. But the bastards what gets me'll have to work for it.'

Stoke nodded.

'If that's the way you want it. What do you think you'll get?'

'Fine. Ten, twenty. Dunno really.'

'Fifty and disqualified is more like it. Come on, let's go,' he said, turning the PC Windsley.

''Ere, just a minute,' Ronnie said suddenly.

'No free advice Sniffer. Get legal aid and make your solicitor rich.'

'No, it's not that. I've got something to tell you and you can't touch me for it neither.'

Ronnie Gleaves spat, aiming for the doorway.

'Yeah, well. I shot something last night what you can't touch me for. A tiger or something it was, like.'

'Watch what you say Ronnie,' his father growled with a meaningful look at Sergeant Stoke.

'Nah, 'sall right Dad. He can't touch me.'

Gleaves turned triumphantly to the sergeant and boasted, 'I shot a tiger and you can't touch me for it. It ain't game nor nothing.'

Constable Windsley could hardly believe what he was hearing. It can't be true, he thought. First old Dan Horrocks sees a big cat that's been run over and now Sniffer Gleaves says he shot a tiger. Sergeant Stoke's voice cut across his thoughts.

'What do you mean you shot a tiger?' he rapped.

Behind him the elder Gleaves sneered.

'There ain't no tiger, nor nothing else neither,' he said. 'People round here thinks they've seen something but there ain't one. They want their heads looking at if you ask me.'

'Nobody is asking you Mr Gleaves,' Stoke barked, 'so stay out of it.'

He questioned Sniffer again.

'Talk. Why did you shoot it?'

Sniffer became defensive.

'Well, maybe I didn't,' he muttered.

'Come on Ronnie, you can't have it both ways. What did you shoot?'

'Well I dunno. It attacked me.'

'Balls.'

Gleaves shuffled his feet again.

'Well it might've done,' he whined. 'It was attacking the chickens.'

'Where?'

'In the yard. Well, down by the fence,' Gleaves lied.

'Where did it come from?'

'I dunno, do I?'

'Where is it now?'

'Ran off over the fields.'

Sergeant Stoke needled him.

'You missed.'

Ronnie Gleaves rose to the bait.

'I didn't, I never miss,' he boasted. ''Course it was a hard shot like. It was going some and it was dark too. Well, nearly. And it had a chicken in its mouth,' he added hastily.

Stoke was still not satisfied.

'Make your mind up,' he said. 'First it ran off. Then you shot it.'

'Well it's wounded anyhow, ain't it. I couldn't miss. It was as big as a cow.'

'Wounded,' Stoke said sharply. 'Are you sure?'

Gleaves licked his lips.

'Yeah, 'course I'm sure. Like I said, I'm a good shot.'

'Gleaves, you're a bloody fool,' was the reply.

Sergeant Stoke was a very worried man. Hearing a noise as they walked across the yard they looked up to see a small yellow aircraft pass overhead. The pilot seemed to be looking down at them but it was too high to be sure. PC Windsley shaded his eyes and waved. Stoke seemed about to say something and then changed his mind.

He broke his silence as they moved out of Gleaves' yard.

'I suppose it had to happen sooner or later. With any luck it'll crawl away and die and that'll be and end to it, but if it doesn't it could turn nasty. It could turn killer. I think that bloody little turd Gleaves is going to have a lot to answer for before very long.'

PC Windsley did not know what to say, and the sergeant did not appear to expect an answer. They drove on in silence.

Chapter 3

Ronnie Gleaves' last dart hit double sixteen to win the game. Ronnie asked his opponent if he wanted to play again.

'Best of three?'

'Not yet. Let's go over with the others. I'll get the drinks in. Same again?'

He collected the empty glasses and Ronnie sniffed loudly, wiping his nose on the same dirty tissue that had been in his pocket for a week or more. Joining a group of youths at a table he shifted an ashtray to make room for his drink. One youth was talking about his new motorcycle, boasting about its speed and his riding skill. Ronnie's darts opponent arrived with two fresh pints of beer and placed them in the space Ronnie had cleared for them.

'Blimey Sid, you still on about that bike?' he said.

He looked round the table and added, 'Sid's still on his first set of L plates and talks like nobody ever had a bike before.'

There was laughter and he continued, 'And he won't be happy until he's fallen off the bloody thing, if he hasn't already.'

Young Sid Newcombe laughed at his own expense, denying that he had ever fallen off his machine.

'For Christ's sake,' another youth complained, 'can't we talk about something else for a change? I'm sick and bloody tired of Sid's bike, last week's football, and what the weather will be like a week on bloody Sunday. For instance,' he added, 'we could talk about when Sid's going to get his round in.'

Sid Newcombe took the hint and fetched two more pints of beer, and threw a packet of crisps on the table. Ronnie Gleaves darts partner took a long pull at his beer.

'You want to hear something different,' he said, 'you listen to what Sniffer told me. Go on Sniffer, you tell them, same as you told me.'

This was the moment Ronnie Gleaves had been waiting for and he savoured it. Little prompting was required to get him to begin his narration, much embellished and with certain facts omitted. There was no false modesty about Ronnie Gleaves.

He finished his tale and with little regard for the truth he answered a host of questions about the animal's size and speed and colour.

The conversation turned to speculation about the origins of the animal, and its identity, and whether the events Ronnie described had ever took place at all. His capacity for exaggeration was well known and it was clear that his story was not being taken seriously, and that nobody believed a single word. Ronnie was righteously indignant. Sid Newcombe summed it up when he declared that he would believe it when he saw it and not a moment before.

The landlord's cry of 'Time, gentlemen, please,' ended the argument and with good humoured bantering at Ronnie's expense the group left the pub.

Sid sat astride his new machine and put on his helmet.

A shout of, 'Watch you don't have to change your name to skid,' got a few laughs. He waved to his pals and roared off into the night.

Pale moonlight shone through a gap in the clouds and the night was pitch black as Sid sped along the narrow road, his gleaming headlamp lighting the way. He loosened his jacket to allow a cooling rush of air to get to him, and he began to feel queasy. He wiped his mouth with the back of his hand and fumbled for the zip of his jacket to do it up again. Maybe he shouldn't have had that last drink, he thought. His insides churned and the motorcycle wobbled. Hell, he felt rough. His mouth filled with saliva and he swallowed hard and tried to spit it away, wiping his mouth again to get the spit off his face. Without warning his stomach contracted violently and he turned his head to one side and spewed foul liquid vomit, which blew onto his coat and half covered his face. Out of control he swerved off the road and ran his machine straight into a tree, smashing his face into the rough bark of the thick trunk. The motorcycle fell back into the road and the engine coughed and died, and then there was silence.

Sid lay unconscious and bleeding. Somewhere an owl hooted.

Green eyes blinked. The thing regarded the youth's still body and inched itself forward, keeping its belly low and favouring its injured paw. The smell of blood was strong in its nostrils and it licked the ruined face and enjoyed the taste. The motorcyclist stirred and moaned, and a low growl came from deep in the animal's throat. Sid opened his remaining good eye and saw a monstrous shape bending over him. A bubble of blood formed on his lips as he opened his mouth in a silent scream that was cut short by a slashing paw. Strong curved teeth sank into his neck. The animal tore his flesh and swallowed the fresh warm meat noisily, the first food it had eaten since its paw was destroyed by Ronnie Gleaves.

An approaching car illuminated the wrecked motorcycle and the white wood of the oak gleamed where the collision had stripped the bark. The car stopped and the driver got out, telling his passenger to stay inside the car. He examined the wreck and looked up as he heard a noise. The female passenger leaned out of the car.

'What is it dear?'

'Looks like a crash. Give me the torch out of the glove box, I think I heard someone.'

Shining the torch at the base of the tree he hesitated. There was a lot of blood. Keeping the torch pointed at the ground he edged cautiously round the trunk. Without warning the thing's eyes were reflected in the beam. It drew back its lips in a snarl. The petrified driver saw it pick something up in its teeth, and then it limped away with an object held in its jaws. Vanishing into the darkness it left only the silence and a mangled body lying at the feet of the terrified driver.

***

Chief Inspector Fillimore leaned forward in his chair and spoke harshly to the sergeant who sat opposite him.

'Sergeant Stoke, I've had a long hard day. I was at this desk until nine o'clock and I don't appreciate being dragged out of bed in the middle of the night because some damned fool thinks he saw a tiger. Was he drunk?' he asked abruptly.

'He didn't say it was a tiger sir, just that it looked like a tiger. He didn't know what it was.'

'Answer the question Sergeant,' Fillimore rapped. 'I asked you if he was drunk.'

'Sir. He was sober, stone cold sober and badly shaken. I got involved because I was doing overtime myself sir.'

He glanced at the hand-written statement that the Chief Inspector had dropped on his desk.

'You've seen what he says,' he continued, 'I had to get one of the traffic boys to drive him and his misses home. He was shaking so much he could hardly stand. The police doctor was here to take a blood sample as it happens, and he gave him a couple of pills to steady him up a bit.'

Fillimore apologised.

'Sorry Sergeant. I didn't mean it to sound like that.'

He read the statement again.

'Hm. Short and to the point. Is that all you could get out of him?'

'I had trouble getting anything at all.'

Fillimore nodded.

'I've read the intelligence report you put in about a large feline animal, as you put it, getting shot. What was his name, Gleaves?'

'That's right sir, Ronald Brian Gleaves. I saw him on Monday and put in an intelligence sheet because of the other report from PC Windsley. That's two positive sightings. Three, after tonight.'

'You think this is the same animal?'

'I bloody well hope so, because if it isn't there must be more than one, and I don't like the sound of that. We're not talking about your average moggie. Anyway, the evidence points to it being the same one.'

Fillimore picked up the phone and spoke to the constable on the other end.

'Get a spare bod to bring up two cups of coffee will you? One spoon in mine and,' he paused as Stoke shook his head, 'no sugar for Sergeant Stoke.'

He put the phone down again.

Stoke pulled a face as he drank the unsweetened coffee.

'I'm afraid we're in for a long night Sergeant. We're going to the hospital as soon as they're ready for us. In the meantime, suppose you tell me what you know about the beast.'

The sergeant thought for a moment.

'Well sir,' he began, 'the cat, or whatever it is, has been popping up for years, on and off. It's been reported more times than I can remember, and the reports cover a wide area. Where it came from in the first place is anyone's guess, but I think it most likely escaped from somewhere. I imagine the usual enquiries were made when it first came to notice, but I've never heard that anyone has come up with anything. There was a picture in the local rag once, some time back, but it must be in the records.'

The Chief Inspector made a note.

'And that's another funny thing,' the sergeant was saying, 'it must be quite old by now, the reports began years ago.'

'What about its size Sergeant? According to Gleaves it was huge. Your witness doesn't say anything about size. Why not? What do you think?'

Sergeant Stoke drank some more coffee before he answered.

'Gleaves is prone to exaggeration sir, to put it in diplomatic language. In other words he's a full time bloody liar. The car driver says he couldn't tell, and I've got that into his statement. Probably though, it's about five feet long, not including the tail. About eight feet overall. It's dark brown, nearly black, and it can run like the clappers. That is, it could before that stupid bastard took a pot shot at it.'

Fillimore looked sharply at the sergeant.

'All right Sergeant, just stick to the facts. Are you telling me you've seen it yourself?'

'Well sir, I think I might have done, about two years ago. I've never been sure,' Stoke replied carefully.

'Did you report it?'

Stoke made a humourless grimace.

'Are you kidding?'

Fillimore put his empty cup on the desk.

'I take your point,' he said.

***

A rubber sheet covered the body that lay on a slab in the middle of the room, and the smell of disinfectant was overlaid by something that made the Chief Inspector's stomach churn. A white-coated figure made notes on an official form, standing up as the policemen entered. He was very tall.

'Come in gents,' he said, 'I've been expecting you. I'm McDermott. I suppose you want to see the body. I ought to warn you it's not pleasant to look at. Frankly, I've never seen anything like it. Are you ready?'

The cover was deftly removed.

Fillimore swore under his breath and tried to ignore what his stomach was doing. The pathetically thin body of the young motorcyclist lay on its back, pale in the harsh light. The head and body was a mass of torn flesh, with deep parallel slashes in lines of four. The left eye socket was empty and leaked a thin trickle of pale fluid into the matted hair. Half the neck was gone and what remained was mutilated. From chest to waist the thin body was a bloody mess, which looked the worse for being washed clean. There was no right arm; the white bone gleamed from where it stuck out of a jagged stump.

Chief Inspector Fillimore missed most of the tall doctor's description of the injuries.

'Leaving out the medical jargon,' McDermott was saying, 'he has been mauled by some animal. As you see, the right arm is missing, partly torn off and partly chewed off. I'm told a cat did it,' he glanced at Fillimore enquiringly, 'and if that's true it was a damn big one. Note the spread of the claw marks.'

McDermott indicated a long diagonal set of tears in the upper chest and ribs.

Fillimore pulled himself together. He was badly affected by the thing on the slab and the stench in the room, but he felt that the doctor expected him to say something.

He said weakly, 'At least he was dead before this happened to him.'

Doctor McDermott shook his head.

'No,' he said quietly, 'he wasn't. He was badly hurt when he crashed his motorcycle but not fatally injured. He died at some stage of whatever happened to him after the crash. It will be in my report. He was mauled to death by something with large claws and sharp teeth, and I only hope it was quick.'

Chief Inspector Fillimore dashed to the sink and hung over it.

Chapter 4

Sitting with the newspaper spread across the kitchen table, PC Windsley read the short account of the death of the motorcyclist, though there was nothing in the article that was new to him. The incident had been the main subject of the morning briefing and Constable Windsley had spent the greater part of the morning touring the schools in his area, warning the children not to approach the animal if they should see it.

Old Dan had been right all along, he mused. There was a big cat after all, and Sniffer Gleaves had shot it, just as he had claimed to have done. What was it Sergeant Stoke had said, something about Gleaves having a lot to answer for, although David was not sure what charges could be brought against him. After all, there was no proof that the two events were connected, was there?

Rita Windsley waved a hand in front of his face, interrupting his chain of thought. He looked across the kitchen table.

'Welcome back,' she said, 'I've been asking you if you wanted more tea, and you were sitting and looking into space.'

'Sorry love,' David apologised, 'I was miles away. Rita, you know on Monday I told you about that cat? How Sniffer Gleaves said he shot it? I suppose you saw this in the paper,' he indicated the column he had been reading, 'I thought Sniffer was just sounding off, he's like that. I wonder what will happen now?'

'I read it, and it's been on the radio too. It will have to be caught, won't it?' Rita Windsley replied.

'Caught or killed. Killed most likely. The marksmen have been put on standby, Stoke is one of them. Sergeant Stoke, I was with him on

Monday after Dan Horrocks told me he'd seen a big cat that was injured. Run over, that was what he thought.'

'Old Dan who brings our milk?'

'That's him, scruffy old guy, always got a two day beard.'

Rita's face clouded.

'It seems such a shame to kill it. It's never done any harm before and it wasn't the cat's fault it was shot, was it? I expect if it hadn't been shot it would have gone its own way. It probably just wants to be left alone.'

'I suppose so. Anyway, I'd better be up and doing or the shops will close before I get there. Do you want anything bringing back?'

Rita thought hard.

'Baby shampoo. Your son and heir knocked the bottle over yesterday and it all spilled out, but it was nearly used up anyway.'

'OK, baby shampoo.'

Rita Windsley was left alone in the kitchen. Two years younger than her husband, she was a tall dark girl with striking blue eyes who had been an airline stewardess before her marriage. She looked out of the window at the hills, which were visible in the distance, and wondered about the fate of the cat. It did seem a shame, but it was frightening to think that there might really be a dangerous animal on the loose. She hoped her David would not be involved in anything dangerous but like most police wives she kept her fears to herself.

A distant aircraft crossed the sky, leaving a long white trail. She wondered if the crew ever thought about the watchers on the ground, as she had done so often during her flying days. She never missed the life as her friend Jenny Wells had when redundancy had brought her flying career to an abrupt end. Jenny had been miserable for months, until she discovered microlight flying and was back in the air within days. Now she flew her own aircraft and had qualified as an instructor. Rita had seen her machine on several occasions and felt happy for her.

***

Two men sat at adjacent desks in the police station. Chief Inspector Fillimore was one, the other was a superintendent from the headquarters staff who had been placed in charge of the operation to find the cat. A red dot on the large wall map marked the spot where the motorcyclist had met his horrible end. A young policewoman made more marks on the map.

When he leaned across to speak to Fillimore the crowns on the superintendent's shoulders caught the light.

'I hear on the grapevine you don't believe we've got a wild cat on our patch Jock,' he said.

Fillimore scowled.

'Some people talk too much. I suppose you heard I threw up in the mortuary too.'

A wide grin spread across the superintendent's face.

'I thought so,' Fillimore said sourly. 'Anyway, the grapevine happens to be wrong, as usual. Half wrong anyway,' he conceded. 'What I saw on the slab would have convinced anyone.'

Picking up a file he continued, 'What puzzles me is why nothing was ever done about it before. It's been around long enough.'

He threw the file back on the desk and a paper that fluttered to the floor was retrieved by the policewoman before she left the room.

The superintendent reached into his briefcase for a curve-stemmed pipe, which he stuffed with coarse tobacco before he talked.

'I can think of one or two good reasons Jock, and one or two that aren't so good. In the first place there has never been any proof that the cat exists. Reports yes, scores of reports, but reports aren't proof. Even if it did exist, what harm was it doing? Knocking off the odd sheep perhaps, but so what? Dogs are a bigger menace by a damn long way. So nobody ever got around to doing anything about it, and why should they? Somebody would have to figure out what to do and how to go about it, which is our baby now. The difference is that now we've got good reason to do something.'

'Shutting the stable door after the horse has gone, sir?'

'Jock, if you ever want to swap those three pips on your shoulder for crowns, don't ever say that where anyone can hear you. I mean that.'

Fillimore looked uncomfortable as the superintendent lit his pipe and threw the spent match at a waste bin, which he missed. Smoking while he talked he continued, ''Nuff said, eh? I'm surprised this is the first time the thing's been seen since you came down from Yorkshire. How long is it, about a year?'

'Eleven months. You know sir, I never realised what a big thing this is. I've got reports that go back years, and this must be just the tip of the iceberg,' he finished, remembering his talk with Sergeant Stoke the previous night.

Tilting his head, the superintendent blew a jet of smoke at the ceiling.

'Likely Jock, very likely,' he agreed.

The ringing telephone on his desk made him sit forward and take the pipe out of his mouth. His expression did not change as he listened to the caller and the only thing he said was 'Yes sir,' as he hung up.

Fillimore waited to be enlightened.

'That was the chief. We're getting a helicopter, not police, it's contracted in. And some sort of cat expert is being sent to, quote, observe and advise, unquote. And there's a press conference this afternoon. I hope I'll have something to say.'

Both men returned to the files on their desks.

***

The wounded paw still throbbed but the pain was not so bad now, more of an aching numbness. The wound was matted with dried blood and gore and the animal licked it carefully, trying to clean itself. The long pink tongue curled around the damaged claws and licked away the sticky matter. A few drops of fresh blood oozed and the animal left them to dry and form a scab over the raw flesh. The injured paw smelled better after the cleaning was done.

Deep in the tangle of undergrowth the cat gnawed the remains of its last meal.

A cheap ring still encircled the dead motorcyclist's finger.

***

Driving rain spattered the windows of the conference room and most of the reporters wore coats. Some were already jotting notes on their pads, others stood and talked. A young woman stood in front of the wall map, getting in the way of a weedy looking photographer who was trying to take a picture. Some seconds elapsed before the arrival of the superintendent was noticed, then everybody started to talk at once. The superintendent held up a large hand and called for silence.

'I am Superintendent Holley,' he introduced himself. 'Some of you know me already. I'll put you in the picture as soon as everybody has found a seat.'

Standing in front of the map he outlined the events that had taken place.

Using a wooden ruler as a pointer he said, 'This is where the motor-cyclist was killed, and the other red spot marks the place where the beast was seen later. It was shot and injured, we believe, here.'

He indicated Gleaves' yard. There was a stir of interest and the reporters took notes.

The superintendent talked for about ten minutes and finished by saying, 'I'm sorry I haven't been able to tell you much but to be honest there isn't a lot to say at present. I'll answer your questions if I can. You sir,' he said, spotting a reporter he knew slightly, 'would you like to begin?'

The question and answer session got under way and Superintendent Holley was asked what he thought the animal was. Before he replied he took his pipe out of his pocket and blew down it noisily, playing for time.

'Good question sir. The answer is that I don't know. I mentioned that an expert on, uh, large felines, has been consulted by this force, and he rightly points out that the beast has never been seen by a qualified observer, but he rules out tigers because everybody knows what a tiger looks like. More than that I can't say. I don't know what it is and that's all there is to it.'

The weedy photographer said something quietly.

'I'm sorry sir, I didn't catch that.'

The photographer looked embarrassed.

'I was just saying that my kids have got a fairy tale book about a witch with a cat. It's called Grimalkin.'

He reddened and fiddled with his camera when laughter broke out.

'Grimalkin, the witch's cat.'

It was the woman who had stood in front of the map when the photographer was trying to take a picture.

She continued, 'Grimalkin sounds like a good name for a killer cat.'

The photographer shot her a look of gratitude. From now on the cat had a name. It was called Grimalkin.

Chapter 5

Rita Windsley rested her head on her husband's bare chest and relaxed as he stroked her hair.

'David,' she whispered.

'Mmm.'

'Let's go somewhere special on Saturday night. I phoned Jenny Wells to baby-sit Steven and she says she will.'

'Mmm.'

'Mmm, yes or Mmm no?'

'Mmm yes. I saw Jenny the other day, from a distance. She flew over the Gleaves' place when I was there with Stoke, in the Red Arrow. I mean, Jenny was in the Red Arrow, not Sergeant Stoke.'

Rita smiled.

'She knows her way round Exmoor like she knows her own back yard. Did you know she gave your sergeant a flight the other day?'

'No, he never said anything, but he wouldn't would he? Have they still got something going?'

Rita brushed a strand of hair out of her eye.

'I think so, on and off. She'll get him sooner or later. Sooner, I think.'

'Stoke!' Windsley exclaimed. 'I never thought of him as the marrying kind.'

'Shows what you know. When he goes he'll go hard, and my money's on Jenny to win.'

David was amused.

'Fancy old Stoke getting hooked.'

'He's not old. Jenny told me he's thirty-five, and I wouldn't call that old. Why don't you call him by his first name?'

David pulled up the cover where it had slipped form her bare shoulders.

'I don't know really,' he replied, 'with some of the sergeants you do and with some you don't. Stoke is one of the don'ts.'

Rita raised herself on one elbow. The coverlet slipped off her shoulders again.

'He is attractive. He could have anyone he wants.'

David raised one eyebrow.

'Anyone? Are you getting ideas?'

'Well, nearly anyone.'

Rita bent and kissed him.

'But it would be safe for the next eight months,' she said softly.

'Huh?'

'I'm pregnant.'

David clasped her tightly.

'Darling are you sure?'

'Sure for two days now. Turn off the light darling, I want to try for twins.'

***

Farmer George Wells worried a lot about his sheep. His flock was only small but he had invested a lot of money in good stock and any losses would hurt him badly, so with his gun under his arm and his collie bitch trotting along beside him he inspected the flock shortly before nightfall. The sheep seemed to be all right and the weather was mild after the rain so he did not want to bring them indoors, but he was nervous about Grimalkin.

The name had caught the public imagination after it was splashed all over the front pages.

His daughter had offered to take her microlight aircraft up at first light and it seemed such a good idea that he had rung round his neighbours, who all asked Jenny to do the same for them. Most knew the pilot of the little yellow aircraft they had become used to seeing, and Mr North was not the only farmer who had received a call from Jenny about a gate left open or a sick animal. They welcomed the idea.

In the meantime George Wells would carry out his inspection on foot, and he hoped that Grimalkin would soon be either captured or killed. In the morning he meant to contact Sergeant Stoke and find out what the police were doing about it. Wells and Stoke often did a bit of rough shooting on the farmer's land.

He hefted the gun under his arm. A pair of young rabbits made a bolt for a nearby copse.

The collie danced around the framer's feet, tail wagging eagerly and looking expectantly at him. He decided to let her have a chase though he knew there was not much chance of her catching them and she would not know what to do if she did. With a wave he sent her on and the dog rushed off, barking joyously. She chased in among the trees and George Wells heard her crashing through the undergrowth and barking for all she was worth. The noise stopped abruptly and she let out an uncertain yelp. Seconds later there was another yelp, then the hysterical barking of a terrified dog, followed by a nightmare screech. There were thrashing noises, then silence.

George Wells trembled as he called the dog's name three times, his numbed brain already accepting that there would be no response from the little collie. He looked round uncertainly, then determined to protect his property, he slipped the safety catch off his gun and crept into the woods.

He found the carcass a dozen yards from the field, lying in the pool of blood that had flowed from the torn throat of the luckless animal.

Jennifer Wells' father was a brave man but no fool. Backing away slowly, he breathed in short gasps. Later he remembered thinking that he must get out into the open where he could not be surprised from behind. In blind useless fury he fired both barrels of his gun in the general direction of the mangled remains of his dog, then ran all the way home and called the police.

Grimalkin had killed again.

***

Sniffer Gleaves halted in the pub car park and switched off the engine of his battered van. As the rattle of the loose exhaust pipe died away he pulled a filthy comb out of his pocket and angled the rear view mirror so that he could see his reflection in the poor light. He made a ragged parting in his unwashed hair and dropped the comb carelessly onto the passenger seat. Crossing the car park he kicked a few loose stones and sniffed loudly.

The loud chatter hushed as soon as he pushed open the door of the public bar. People nudged their neighbours and muttered quiet words. A group that included some of his drinking mates got up and pushed past him roughly, not speaking as they went out of the door. With falling confidence he asked the barmaid for a pint of beer and she looked towards the landlord and shook her head dumbly. The landlord elbowed her out of the way and glared at Sniffer with undisguised hostility.

'You'd better get out of here,' he said roughly, 'folks are blaming you for young Sid. His dad's been in here looking for you and I'm not having any trouble with your sort. Get out!'

Sniffer bit his lip and kept quiet, and left the pub with his face burning with a mixture of anger and shame.

Without warning a fist hit him on the side of his head, knocking him to the ground. Boots thudded into him from all directions and his nose spurted blood as he tried to cover his head with his arms. A vicious kick in the ribs forced the air out of his lungs and he struggled for breath, unable to cry out. More kicks and punches followed, then there was the sound of mocking laughter. Footsteps crunched on the gravel as his assailants ran off into the night.

Chapter 6

The insistent buzz of the alarm clock woke Rita Windsley without disturbing her husband. She reached over him and turned it off. The time was seven o'clock. Rita let her hair brush David's face.

'David, the alarm's gone off. Time to wake up.'

He opened his eyes and brushed her hair off his face.

'Uh uh. What time is it?'

'Seven o'clock. Steven is still asleep.'

'OK, thanks. We can lie in for a while, I'm not on until nine. I wish I was having my Saturday rest day though. Shall I try to grab an extra shift tomorrow as well? There's plenty of overtime going because of this Grimalkin thing. All that lovely money.'

Rita smiled.

'You can spend it on me, and my daughter when I have her. I'm going out later too, I called Jenny Wells yesterday and she's baby-sitting for Steven tonight so I'm driving over to pick her up at eleven and we'll do a bit of shopping and she'll have her tea with us. Well, Steven and me. You said you won't be in until about six so I'll fix something while you get ready. Will that be all right?' she asked anxiously. 'I mean it's not much but I didn't know you were going to be working today.'

David smiled at her.

'Neither did I love. I won't want a lot when I come in, not if we're going out. A couple of fish fingers will do.'

Rita kissed him, then threw back the cover on her side of the bed and padded barefoot to the window, peeking past the drawn curtain.

'It's going to be a nice day. I'll look in on Steven and then I'm coming back to bed.'

The child was fast asleep, clutching a grubby furry toy. Rita tried without success to prise it from his grasp. Not wanting to wake him, she let go of the toy and let him sleep on, adjusted his covers and closed the door quietly.

David had his eyes closed. She slipped back into bed beside him.

'Fooled you,' David whispered in her ear, covering one of her breasts with his hand.

'Beast,' she whispered back, and covered his hand with her own.

She rolled over to meet him.

***

Grimalkin, the witch's cat, was weak and tired. Surprised by farmer George Wells' collie it had killed quickly and efficiently but the victory had been costly and more damage had been done to the broken paw, which oozed blood. It throbbed painfully as Grimalkin slunk through the tangled scrub. The cat held the paw clear of the ground and lashed its long tail angrily. The slitted green eyes burned with hate.

***

'Come in!' Superintendent Holley bellowed in response to a knock on the door of the Incident Room. A civilian wearing a tweed suit entered. The Superintendent put his pipe and stood up.

To Chief Inspector Fillimore he said, 'Jock, I'd like you to meet Mr Cole. He's an authority on cats.'

The civilian frowned slightly at this description of himself. Fillimore extended his hand.

'Jock Fillimore. Glad to meet you. I hope you can help us with this business, we're up against something outside our experience.'

Mr Cole cleared his throat.

'I hope I can be of some assistance,' he replied.

'Mr Cole arrived last night after you had gone off duty, Jock,' Superintendent Holley informed the chief inspector, 'and he went straight out to the Wells' place where the dog was killed. Here, where the map is marked.'

He said to Cole, 'As you see, we have four positive sightings. The cat was shot here, in Gleaves' yard. On Monday morning it was seen by a local man at location number two on the map. Number three is the spot where the motorcyclist was killed, and number four you know about already, the Wells farm. That was last night and I don't mind telling you I'm stuck for ideas.'

Cole laid his briefcase on the table and removed a large brown envelope.

'Perhaps I can add a little something,' he said as he shook out some photographs.

'These are pictures I took last night. I've spent most of the night doing a post-mortem on the dog.' He selected a photograph. 'Here is the dog as we found it, lying on its left side you will notice. The throat wound is what killed it. That was caused by a bite, as you might have expected. As I might have expected,' he corrected himself. He continued, 'The interesting thing is the right flank, here,' Cole used a pencil to indicate a wound. 'That was done by a claw. I measured the length and depth of the injury and from those measurements I've been able to make a tentative calculation, more of a guess really, about the size of the animal that inflicted the wound. It has a reach of about twenty inches. The wound was caused by the animal digging its claws into the dog and pulling it back in a raking motion,' Cole demonstrated. 'The depth of the wound and the distance between the claw marks tells me quite a lot. I should have expected the wound to be deeper than it actually is, this is quite superficial when compared to the damage that a big cat usually does. I was puzzled until I turned the dog over.'

Cole stopped for breath and selected a second photograph.

'This is the left flank. There are no injuries but look here, where I'm pointing.'

He moved the tip of his pencil in a circular motion.

'This patch here, it's a bit faint on the photo I'm afraid, this is blood and scab matter. I believe the dog fell onto the cat's injured paw and opened up the gunshot wound.'

Cole stopped for breath again.

'What else do we know? I spoke to that sergeant last night, Harry Stoke, and asked for his opinion about the size of the cat.'

Both policemen looked surprised by Mr Cole's use of Sergeant Stoke's first name. They must have hit it off, the superintendent thought.

Cole continued to speak.

'We agree about the body size, about five feet. Secondly...'

'Just a minute Mr Cole,' Fillimore interrupted, 'I'm trying to get this on paper.'

Cole waited for a nod from the chief inspector before he spoke again.

'Secondly then, the weight of the cat. Hard to say but my guess, and I stress the word guess, is that it might be in the region of one hundred and twenty pounds.' He waited for Fillimore to finish writing and continued, 'We can be more certain about the next few items. Fact one,' he enumerated on his finger, 'the animal is badly injured in the right forepaw. Fact two, the wound is suppurating and causing discomfort. Mobility is impaired, perhaps severely. Fact three, the cat is weak.'

Fillimore laid his pen down and flexed his cramped fingers.

'Mr Cole, can I ask a question?'

'Certainly.'

'How weak is it? Is there any chance it will crawl under a hedge and die?'

Cole considered the question.

'Unlikely. There are one or two things in its favour. Look at the map.'

The door opened and Sergeant Stoke entered. His 'Morning sir,' included both the senior policemen, who were taken by surprise when he addressed Mr Cole as Peter. With a start Chief Inspector Fillimore realised that up until then Cole had not offered his first name.

'Good morning Harry. We're discussing the cat's chances of crawling away and dying somewhere.'

He turned his attention to the map again.

'Look here. Water. In terms of survival water is more important than food, and there is no shortage of water.'

Sergeant Stoke agreed. Superintendent Holley sounded excited.

'That's where it is then! Jock, hand me that marker pen. Somewhere near to where it was last night, and not far from water!'

He drew a circle round the Wells' farm. Cole shook his head.

'I wish it was that simple. I'm inclined to agree that the cat is likely to be inside that circle, but it might not be. It has something else in its favour. Would anyone care to guess what that might be?'

When nobody else answered Stoke spoke up.

'I think I might know what you're getting at from something you said last night. It's a cat, right?'

Peter Cole beamed.

'Right. Cats are the toughest, most independent, single-minded survivor types in the animal kingdom. They never know when they are beaten. Predicting what this one will do next is a waste of time.'

'Peter, we have to try,' Stoke pleaded.

'I know, and I am trying. I agree with Superintendent Holley that the cat is somewhere on the Wells' property and I said as much to Mr Wells earlier this morning. Which reminds me, he said something that I didn't grasp, that you and Miss Wells were in the Red Arrow. I'm afraid I didn't understand.'

Stoke explained.

'It's an aircraft, a microlight actually, and this one happens to be yellow. We flew around the farm, hers and a few others, to see if there were any signs of the cat. Or where it had been,' he added grimly.

'What did you see?' Fillimore exclaimed.

Stoke shrugged his shoulders.

'Not much,' he admitted. 'I'm no expert of course, but it takes a lot of experience to see properly from the air, the angles aren't what you're used to. Jenny, Miss Wells that is, sees more than I do and she knows Exmoor like the back of her hand, but she says that in a week or so it won't be possible to see through the trees because the leaves will have grown that much. I could see what she meant but I think an aerial survey will be useful all the same. I've asked her to take me up again tomorrow.'

Superintendent Holley nodded vigorous agreement.

'Well done Sergeant, very well done. I wouldn't mind a bash at that myself. I've often wondered who that thing belonged to, if it's the same one I see from my garden now and again. It looks like damn good fun to me!'

***

Flying that morning had not been damn good fun. Sergeant Stoke had arrived at the Wells' farm to find Jenny and her parents walking towards their house, returning from an inspection of their flock. It emerged that George Wells had spent the whole night on watch near the place where his sheep dog had been savagely killed. Looking strained and unshaven he unloaded his shotgun outside the house. Jenny and her mother went indoors while the men talked.

Neither had much to say. Each had spent a sleepless night. Eventually Harry Stoke broke the silence.

'Sorry about the dog George.'

'Me too,' Wells said morosely. 'Anyway, Grimalkin stayed away last night, most likely it was scared off by the rushing round and the flashlights and all. I'll be bringing the sheep inside tonight and every night from now on, and I'll be doing the rounds all day.'

Stoke thought the farmer ought to get some sleep but it would have been pointless to say so.

Jenny popped her head out of the window to tell them that a pot of tea was made and getting cold. Sitting round the kitchen table, nobody had much to say. It had all been said the night before. Jenny left the kitchen and returned shortly, wearing her yellow flying clothing, and she dumped Stoke's gear on the table. While he struggled into it Mrs Wells took his jacket and hung it up.

'Loose articles?' Jenny asked.

Stoke was annoyed with himself for forgetting to empty his pockets. His fumblings produced a small pile of coins and his car keys. He ought to have remembered that Jenny had a thing about loose articles and the consequences of dropping things in aircraft. He wondered if all pilots were like that, and decided they probably were. There was more to being a pilot than he had thought, and Jenny claimed to be one of the best. By the little things, her attention to details and her precise flying, she had proved it more than once. Harry Stoke was glad she was not pushy about it. Perhaps that was another mark of a good pilot.

As soon as she was satisfied with her pre-take off checks Jenny increased the engine power and the yellow microlight was soon airborne. Jenny allowed a slight crosswind to drift them over a small stand of trees before she altered her heading and began her patrol.

Stoke wondered if he should have brought binoculars, then decided they would be impossible to use while wearing goggles, and hard to hold with the wind rushing past the open cockpit. Everything on the ground seemed quiet. Jenny circled her own farm while she gained height, then set course for her nearest neighbours.

On Mr North's land a cowherd waved. Jenny dipped her wing in acknowledgement and wrote something on her kneepad. Stoke saw people in four other fields and noticed they all carried shotguns. One farmer waved from his cab as he did the rounds in his Landrover.

They had been airborne for about an hour when Jenny began to climb. The engine note deepened as she applied power and the horizon dropped away. When she levelled out Stoke could see the vast expanse of Exmoor spread out below. They circled, Stoke closing his eyes for a second when the low sun shone directly at him during the turn.

Spotting a helicopter with red markings on a green background far below Stoke wondered if Jenny had deliberately turned to show the profile of her aircraft to its best advantage.

Exmoor seemed so big, such a large area, the hilly country rolling into the distance. If Grimalkin should go into open country and lie low, which Stoke considered likely, he wondered how the beast would ever be captured. Or killed. Stoke shivered in the open cockpit.

Feeling uneasy, he wondered where they were. To the north he could see the Bristol Channel and a couple of ships. That was not much help. The channel was north of the whole of Exmoor. He tried again and found a road that seemed promising. The B3224 ran east/west between Exford and Simonsbath, so if he could find Dunkery Beacon, which was the highest point on Exmoor, then... he noted with surprise that they had descended without him realising it. The aircraft banked slightly and straightened on a new heading. Jenny maintained the descent and her father's farm appeared in front of them. She throttled right back, raised the nose slightly, and skimmed the grass so gently that Stoke hardly felt the wheels make contact with the ground.

The wind had increased slightly. Stoke unstrapped and vacated the aircraft, then held one wingtip while Jenny taxied to her hangar at walking pace. He noticed that he walked with a slight sailor's roll as a result of the slight swaying motion of the microlight during the flight. The feeling was odd but not unpleasant.

Jenny killed the engine. Removing her helmet, she shook her hair so that it fell about her shoulders, and they wheeled the aircraft inside.

After noticing the time Stoke declined Mrs Wells' offer of breakfast with regret because he was due on duty shortly. Jenny confessed that she hadn't intended to remain airborne for so long, and she had climbed and flown aimlessly just to get away from it all.

'Wouldn't we all like to do that,' her mother declared with feeling.

Jenny accompanied Harry Stoke to his car, Stoke remembering his keys and his money when he was half way out of the door and having to go back for them. He squeezed her hand.

'Don't worry about me missing breakfast. I'll get something later.'

'I can't stay out here for more than a minute,' Jenny said, 'I must phone Mr North, he was a cow short this morning unless I miscounted, and I have to ring Rita Windsley. She's supposed to pick me up this morning but I think I'll meet her in town instead.'

She brushed his lips with hers and walked slowly back indoors.

***

Superintendent Holley filled his pipe and lit it. His match missed the metal waste bin and joined the spent matches that littered the floor. Chief Inspector Fillimore contemplated the red circle that the superintendent had drawn around the Wells' farm.

'How fast can it move?' he asked abruptly.

Peter Cole looked pleased with the question.

'The fastest land animal in the world is a cat. The cheetah can manage over seventy miles per hour over short distances. Over seventy miles per hour,' he repeated blissfully. 'The cheetah, by the way, is the only cat which can't retract its claws. Of course, all the felines can move fast if need be.' His face darkened. 'But not on three legs and in a weakened condition. I think Grimalkin can only manage a slow walk. Say about half the pace of a walking man.'

The superintendent thought about that.

'So allowing for sleep and injuries, about twenty-five miles in twenty-four hours would be about right, do you think?'

Cole hesitated while he worked out the calculation.

'That would be about it, but don't forget what I said about all the cats. I wouldn't put it past Grimalkin to have a few surprises left.'

Fillimore had another question.

'Excuse me sir, but there is one thing which bothers me,' he said.

Cole's expression was unreadable.

'I was wondering, I don't know much about these things, but I wondered whether Grimalkin is dangerous. To people, I mean. What I'm trying to say is that we know, well we think that the motorcyclist who was killed was partially eaten by the cat. We didn't tell the boy's parents but we never found the missing arm. So you see...'

When Cole swung round from the map and faced Fillimore the superintendent thought he had never seen anyone so angry.

'Get to the point man!' he shouted. 'I wondered which one of you was going to ask! Well all right. The answer is yes, dammit. Yes it is dangerous. It's bloody dangerous, and it could kill again. And all because some bloody fool, some lunatic with a gun, some... some imbecile with an itchy trigger finger. He ought to be locked up! He ought to be bloody well hung! I'd do it myself! I'd, I'd, I'd...' he sputtered into silence.

Now we know whose side he's on, the superintendent thought. Things are starting to get very interesting. I've never actually seen a man tear his hair before.

Chapter 7

The spring weather had brought the whole population out into the streets. Rita Windsley met Jennifer Wells outside the Post Office as they had arranged on the telephone and they spent two hours window shopping and making small purchases. Rita wheeled the pushchair along the crowded pavements while eleven month old Steven clutched the grubby toy that he would not be without.

They were lucky to find an empty table in the little teashop they had discovered some months previously. Rita sat Steven on her lap and the boy played with his beloved toy while they ordered tea and biscuits. Rita selected a large sticky doughnut.

Jennifer Wells looked envious and declared that she too would like one but it would go straight to her hips if she did.

Rita leaned towards her and whispered, 'Don't tell anybody but I'm eating for two. You're the first to know. I've been dying to tell you.'

'Rita, that's wonderful!' Jenny exclaimed loudly, then clapped her hand over her mouth. Some customers looked disapproving. Jenny giggled and whispered, 'I'm so pleased for you! How long have you known? I can't wait to hear all about it.'

'Only a few days, I've only just caught. Steven,' she said severely, 'give me that disgusting animal. Eat this biscuit and do try not to get more than half of it on your face, there's a good boy.'

Steven reluctantly exchanged his toy for a biscuit and proceeded to make a mess with it.

'Do you want a boy or a girl?' Jenny asked.

Rita patted her stomach proudly.

'This one's a girl,' she said. 'David has got his son, this little terror,' she hugged him, 'and now I'm going to have my daughter. Or twins,' she said mischievously, and whispered in her friend's ear.

Jennifer tried to stifle her laughter behind her hand when she heard what Rita had said about trying for twins. She received more disapproving glares.

'Ssh,' Rita said, 'and don't look now but a friend of yours has just walked in.'

Jennifer spun round quickly and blushed to the roots of her hair when she saw the knowing look on her friend's face. Steven Windsley regarded Harry Stoke with round solemn eyes as the sergeant sat down.

'You said I might find you here. Mind if I join you? Is everything all right at home?' he asked Jennifer.

Jenny's face clouded.

'Rita,' she said, 'we had some trouble last night.' Her voice shook. 'I didn't want to tell you and spoil your news but last night that horrible cat killed daddy's dog. He's ever so upset, and so am I.'

'Jenny, you should have said something!' Rita exclaimed.

She laid her hand on the other girl's wrist.

'I went out to Jenny's place last night with a civilian chap who knows about cats,' Stoke explained. 'Actually I've just popped into the library before I go back to the police station and I've picked up a book he wrote.'

He placed the book on the table. It was entitled, 'The World's Big Cats,' by P F Cole.

Young Steven Windsley wriggled on his mother's lap and tried to grasp the book, attracted by the picture on the glossy cover.

'Pussy,' he said.

Rita pushed the book out of his sticky reach.

'Bad pussy,' she said.

'Bad pussy,' the little boy repeated solemnly.

Harry Stoke picked up the book and stood up.

'Better not stop, I'm on duty soon. I'll say hello to David for you Rita, I'll be in his car all afternoon, and Jenny, I'll see you later perhaps. I'm hiding in your place tonight with a couple of marksmen in case Grimalkin comes back. 'Bye, young Steven.'

Rita and Jennifer both looked very thoughtful as Sergeant Stoke left the teashop.

***

Mr Cole and Chief Inspector Fillimore made up their differences after lunch, but before the afternoon session with the media who had been clamouring for information something happened which put them back on opposite sides of the fence.

Cole had brought some special equipment with him, including a short rifle that fired tranquillising darts. When he announced his intention to stun and capture the animal Fillimore was furious, and Superintendent Holley hardly less so, though more restrained.

'I don't think you understand mister,' he said harshly, 'I want that thing dead, do you hear? Dead! I don't give a damn for scientific interest, I want Grimalkin's hide nailed to a wall! I can't stop you, I've had the chief on my back already, but let me tell you this - if you interfere in any way with my marksmen I'll charge you with obstructing the police in the execution of their duty and I'll lock you up myself. I hope I make myself clear.'

Cole was not intimidated.

'Abundantly clear, Superintendent, your objections are noted,' he said coldly, and turned his back on both policemen. Fillimore counted slowly to ten and Cole was out of the door before he reached eight.

'Simmer down Jock,' Holley advised. 'I feel the same as you do but I can see his point of view, and let's be honest with ourselves, we need him.'

Fillimore glared.

'I'm not convinced sir,' he said stiffly.

Superintendent Holley employed his tactic of gaining time by lighting his pipe while Fillimore waited impatiently.

After missing the bin with his spent match he said at last, 'Look at it this way Jock, we haven't got much on our side. We can't put constables out to beat around the moors for Grimalkin, think of the risk. All that would get us would be a dead copper, and we both know it. We can't cover the whole of Exmoor with marksmen either, unless you call one marksman for every ten square miles adequate coverage. It won't do Jock. Cole is an expert, he can find the cat if anyone can, and it doesn't matter who gets there first. If we do, the cat is dead. If he does it goes in the cage. Either way it's out of our hair.'

He held up a large meaty hand.

'Having said that, I intend to get there first. Starting tomorrow there will marksmen out in Landrovers. They'll be able to go anywhere in a hurry, and there will be a marksman in the helicopter. That will be Stoke, he's a marksman and he's trained for airborne work. The helicopter is operating from a school playing field for want of somewhere better and I want that it in the air all day long from now on, every day, until this operation is over. I'll be in the Mobile Incident Room with a fast car handy, and I want you on the radio link. I need someone senior there. Sign out a pistol as soon as we've finished with the press people. Let's go to it!'

The police officers and Peter Cole put on a united front at the press conference. The matter of their differences of opinion was carefully avoided. Superintendent Holley again provided details of the events that had taken place and summarised the intentions of his force and the methods he would use. Chief Inspector Fillimore asked them to print a prepared appeal not to venture on the moors, the warning to include the whole of Exmoor.

'The warning will be broadcast on the news tonight,' he informed them, 'and it cannot be repeated too often. Grimalkin is dangerous and may attack again.'

Peter Cole found that he had to deliver a lecture to his audience, some of whom had obviously done some reading. He began by replying to a question.

'There are as many as forty different species of wild cats,' he informed his listeners. 'I'll ignore all but two for the time being, but first I want to make some general comments. All cats can swim, though most prefer not to if they can avoid it. They can all climb trees, and some species habitually drag their prey into a tree to eat it. You may have heard that lions can't climb. Well, they can. Cats are fast runners, at least over short distances. Other qualities they have are strength, camouflage, and intelligence. Most cats are nocturnal hunters, but not all of them. So much for generalisations.'

'What kind of cat is Grimalkin?'

The question came from the woman who had been present at the first conference, which Cole had not attended, and who had come out in support of the photographer who had given the cat its name.

'I'm coming to that,' Cole replied. 'I said I would concentrate on two cats in particular. First, the leopard. This cat can weigh as much as a well-built man, say fourteen or fifteen stones. Most experts, myself included, consider the leopard to be the most dangerous of the big cats, although it isn't the biggest. It's a great climber and it can tackle trees and rocky places which most animals would find impossible. It can jump forty feet, and pound for pound it's probably the strongest of the cats. It can pull a carcass twice its own weight into a tree.'

'An Exmoor pony for instance?'

'Yes madam, or a deer, or even a human being. If Grimalkin is a leopard I think it reasonable to assume it has killed both ponies and deer in the past, along with birds and sheep and other animals including dogs. I don't know how many dogs are lost on Exmoor every year but I imagine that quite a few have fallen victim to Grimalkin in the past. Last night's killing was not a first for the cat, you can be sure of that. As it happens, leopards seem to have a taste for dog flesh. They also have a reputation as scavengers, so all things considered no leopard on Exmoor would ever go hungry, nor would it come to harm, except by accident. And there's another thing,' Peter Cole added ominously, 'they are very easily roused if they are disturbed.'

He stopped to pour water into a paper cup, and there was a buzz of excitement. Cole gestured for silence and resumed his talk.

'I'll leave the leopard for a while, thought I shall have more to say about him later. The other big cat I want to discuss is the jaguar, one of the largest cats. The jaguar is an American, mainly South America, but not unknown in parts of the United States, though I personally have never seen one there. It is nocturnal, very active, and extremely aggressive. I said it is big; it can weigh up to two hundred and fifty pounds. Its ability to climb is on a par with the leopard's and it swims more readily than most cats. As it happens, fish are part of its diet. As I mentioned, it is nocturnal, but not wholly, it is often active during the day. It guards its territory jealously and it's more likely to fight than run, and a fight with a jaguar only ends one way. Most human beings who have been attacked by jaguars probably provoked the animals by trespassing on what they regard as their own ground. Jaguars tend to see domestic livestock as their own property too, and it isn't unknown for herdsmen to be attacked. Sheep and cattle farmers please note. Wounded jaguars have a nasty habit of doubling back and turning the tables on their attackers. You may think you know what relentless means but believe me ladies and gentlemen, an injured cat bent on revenge gives a whole new meaning to the word.'

The water in his paper cup was warm and tasted waxy. Peter Cole made an expression of distaste as he put the cup down. A reporter in the front row took advantage of the pause to ask a question.

'Do you think Grimalkin is one of these, a leopard or jaguar?' He looked doubtful. 'I thought they had spots but isn't Grimalkin supposed to be black?'

Mr Cole thanked him for the question.

'One of the curious things about jaguars and leopards is that melanism, that is to say black or near black pelts, is quite common, and this is what makes me think Grimalkin is one of these two. Certainly as regards size and colour the fit is good.'

'What about panthers and pumas?' someone asked.

'Panther is another name for leopard and don't let anyone tell you different,' Cole replied dryly. 'The word black panther is commonly used and it's often supposed, quite wrongly, that it is a different species.'

'That's taught me a thing or two,' the reporter admitted, 'but what about pumas?'

'Good question. The Beast of Exmoor, as it was known before it was called Grimalkin, has often been identified as a puma. Not by experts I hasten to add. The other names for puma are cougar, mountain lion, and, yet again, panther. Those are the common names, there are others. Fascinating beast, the puma. It's another American. It gets top marks for its ability to adapt to any condition, it can live in jungles, in mountains, and in deserts, and a recent trend is urbanisation in some parts of the United States. It weighs up to two hundred pounds, which puts it in the right bracket for the Beast of Exmoor, but I rule it out because of its colour and because it does a bunk if anyone comes near, unless it has cubs. It isn't often dark and the fact is, it's hard to know if there are pumas in the area or not.'

'Is it any less dangerous?'

'Less dangerous that what? If you rub any of the big cats up the wrong way the result is the same. Is being killed by a jaguar any less dangerous than being killed by a leopard? The question has no meaning. I can't say this often enough, and the chief inspector has said it too, that thanks to that lunatic who shot Grimalkin we're dealing with the most dangerous animal there is, a wounded big cat. Whatever Grimalkin is, and my first choice is a leopard, it's unbelievably dangerous. There's no telling where it will strike next, but strike it will, unless something is done first. Whatever that something is,' Cole concluded grimly.

Knowing what he meant, neither police officer looked pleased. It suddenly dawned on Chief Inspector Fillimore that Peter Cole was an extremely brave man, who knew the appalling risks better than anybody and was still prepared to approach Grimalkin with a short range weapon of doubtful efficacy and try to get his shot in first. Fillimore began to see him in a different light.

The reporters hastened out of the building and Superintendent Holley let out a weary groan.

'Jock,' he ordered, 'draw your pistol out of the armoury now and stay here till I get back. I want Mr Cole to come with me. Starting now, I want either you or me in this building at all times until the operation begins tomorrow. Kip down for a bit if you like, but be here. Understood?'

'Got it sir. This'll cost me a new spring outfit for the misses.'

'Me too,' Holley agreed. 'Do what I do and fiddle your expenses,' he joked feebly. 'See you after we've had a bite to eat, eh?'

Superintendent Holley and Mr Cole left the building in the wake of the reporters.

Fillimore telephoned his wife from his own office and then used the station facilities to wash and shower. He was in bare feet with his shirt outside his trousers when a policewoman from the duty room burst in.

***

Cole slumped wearily into his seat as Superintendent Holley drove expertly through the afternoon traffic. He was tired, they all were, though heaven knew they had good cause. He jerked to wakefulness when the superintendent spoke.

'I won't have you and Chief Inspector Fillimore at each other's throats all the time Mr Cole. I've spoken to him already and now I'm telling you. The chief has asked me, no, told me, to cooperate with you right down the line and I will, but there are limits and both of you are pushing your luck, so back off. I won't tolerate a pair of prima donnas. Have you got that?'

Cole accepted the rebuke.

'Sorry, I let my feelings get the better of me. Superintendent, what sort of man is he, the one who shot Grimalkin?'

Superintendent Holley snorted. 'He's everything you said he is. Ronald Brian Gleaves is his name, alias Sniffer, even his father calls him

Sniffer sometimes. Born loser, he got his record office number for his eighteenth birthday. Never committed a decent offence, he hasn't the wit, but always in minor trouble of some sort, usually traffic offences and poaching. He lives with his father who, incidentally, hasn't much time for him. His latest stunt was to pour about fifty gallons of dirty petrol down a wastepipe in the old man's workshop, according to information given to me by Sergeant Stoke. Mention of Stoke reminds me, Sniffer's got himself a Sheba.'

'What's that?'

'Alsatian bitch. They're nearly always called Sheba, don't ask me why. Shout Sheba in your local park to the next ten Alsatian bitches you see, and nine of them will come running.'

Talking to himself as much as to Cole the superintendent continued, 'Sniffer's old man is a funny old bugger with a machinery repair business. By all accounts he does a damn good job, he seems to have had a good apprenticeship at some time. He really did his best for Sniffer but he was casting his pearls before swine and he gave up eventually. Sniffer takes after his mother. God what a bitch she was! She ran the poor old bugger ragged and then she disappeared, ran off to the bright lights of London, leaving the old man holding the baby, young Sniffer, who was about eight at the time. Anyway, that finished off the old man. Now he keeps himself to himself and never goes anywhere except to see his widowed sister in Bristol every fourth Saturday. He mends her washing machine, changes the light bulbs, stuff like that, and spends the night over there, comes back early Sunday morning. Not much of a life.'

Mr Cole grunted his agreement and settled deeper into the passenger seat.

Chapter 8

Rita drove her car behind Jennifer's. She had told Jenny that she would cancel her night out with David but Jenny would not hear of it. Rita must have her celebration, she insisted. Steven Windsley slept soundly, strapped into his chair on the rear seat and clutching his toy animal.

Rita negotiated the heavy traffic and soon they were in the countryside. The new leaves on the trees that lined the road looked nice, she thought as she glanced sideways, and she wound the window down, taking care that the baby was not disturbed by the draught.

Turning into a farm lane she saw a man working on the far side of a strip of rough grass. Farmer George Wells had begun to clear the strip about a year previously and he usually managed to spend half a day each week hacking the tangle of thorny bushes and brambles and burning it when he had a sizeable pile. Blue smoke from a dying bonfire curled into the air and the marks of his old fires were visible. Coarse grass was growing over them.

Steven woke as the car stopped. Rita carried him in the crook of her arm as she walked towards the farmer, who stopped work and laid down his billhook, and wiped his brow with a large floral handkerchief.

'Hello you two,' he greeted them. 'Have a good time in town? Hello baby Steven.'

The chuckling infant grasped the horny finger he held up.

'He's getting big isn't he? Set him down on the grass, here where it's dry, he must be heavy. Let him play around a bit.'

'He is heavy,' Rita admitted. 'I'd better fetch his furry friend from the car. He loves the smelly thing.'

Jennifer Wells volunteered to fetch the boy's toy. Steven sat on the grass and played happily.

'Jennifer told me about your dog Mr Wells. I'm so sorry.'

The farmer looked grave.

'Aye, she was a good dog. They took a lot of photos last night before they took her away. It was a chap in plain clothes who did it, not one of your David's lot. Jennifer's sergeant came with him. He told me Grimalkin probably sleeps all day and hunts at night or dusk, like foxes and badgers. He said probably, but not necessarily, he said he didn't know for sure. I'm putting the sheep in the paddock tonight. I don't like it, I can tell you.'

Rita agreed.

'I know. They're asking all the police to work overtime until it's caught. David says they're running about like headless chickens but I don't think he's been involved yet. I hope he doesn't have to.'

They stood and chatted while the boy sat on the grass and played. He chuckled happily to himself and held up his toy towards the tangle of brambles.

'Bad pussy. Bad pussy,' he said solemnly.

The adults smiled indulgently.

'Bad pussy,' Rita repeated.

Farmer Wells asked Rita if she had ever seen a wren's nest.

'I found one this morning. They make little round balls of stuff with just a small hole in the side to get in. Like this,' he said, cupping his hands together. 'They make their nests so well that this one has lasted through from last year. I'll leave that bit alone and maybe they'll be back this year too. There's still enough of this jungle to work on. About ten acres it seems to me.'

Jennifer Wells laughed.

'Father you lie. Last week you told me it's a mere half acre. No,' she added seriously, 'I've never seen one, have you Rita? Let's go and see. We won't disturb the birds though, will we?'

The farmer shook his head.

'No, they're not back yet, that's if they do come back, I don't know of they do or not, but we won't get too close. Over here.'

He led the way.

Rita called, 'Stay there Stevie, there's a good boy. Mummy's not going away.'

The boy chewed the ear of his furry animal.

They admired the tiny nest the wrens had built, the women standing on tiptoe for a better look. The birds had woven a ball of fluff into the bushes and made it secure, and they were able to see the small hole in the side. It looked very safe and snug and they hoped the birds would return and raise another family of young.

When Jennifer had seen enough she turned and started to walk away. Suddenly she uttered a stifled scream. George Wells spun round as she stood transfixed with horror, pointing with a shaking hand at the dark slinking creature which crawled on its belly towards the innocently playing child. It lunged forward and sank its teeth into the boy's shoulder, and dragged the screaming infant into the tangled scrub.

Wells shouted, 'It's Grimalkin, it's the cat!' and Rita dashed towards it, crying, 'Stop it, stop it, oh my baby! Stop it!'

The animal dragged the loudly screaming infant into the tangle of thorns and brambles.

Rita plunged after it, still crying, 'Stevie, Stevie, come back, come back!'

Thousands of viciously sharp thorns tore her skin and blood ran into her eyes and she blinked it away unnoticed as she fought to reach her baby son.

Wells was galvanised into action.

'Jenny, get up to the house and call an ambulance. Hurry girl, hurry!'

He snatched up his short curved billhook and chopped frantically at the brambles behind the struggling girl, trying desperately to reach her.

The pitiful screams of the little boy died away.

***

Chief Inspector Fillimore grabbed the phone and snapped, 'Don't do anything! I'm on my way down!'

Flinging the girl aside he raced along the corridor and seconds later he burst into the control room, still barefooted. Two radio operators sat at their consoles, a civilian and a white faced young constable. The control room sergeant spoke in urgent tones.

'I thought I'd better call you first sir. The hospital phoned just now and they've got PC Windsley's wife in there. She's been attacked by the cat and they say she's a bit of a mess.'

Fillimore sized up the situation quickly.

'Where is Windsley now?' he demanded.

'Out with Sergeant Stoke. She was on his patch too. I hope...'

'All right.' Fillimore cut him off. 'Why the hell didn't the hospital call us before? No, never mind that. Get me Stoke on the radio, quickly.'

He turned to the radio operators.

'If either of you say one word about this on the air you'll be looking for new jobs in the morning. Are we on talk through?'

The civilian replied.

'No sir, I took it off as soon as I heard. I thought if somebody else got the message and radioed in it would be best if PC Windsley didn't hear it, so I'm relaying all calls through the board now. If anyone does radio in nobody can hear it.'

'Good man.' Fillimore praised him, 'That was good thinking. Well done.'

The control room sergeant interjected.

'I tried to call Sergeant Stoke sir, but he was out of the car. I spoke to PC Windsley and let him think he wasn't getting through on his car radio. I told him to get Sergeant Stoke to ring in from a public call box.'

The telephone rang as he finished speaking. The uniformed constable snatched it up and swivelled his chair round.

'Sir, I've got Sergeant Stoke now.'

Fillimore took the phone from him.

'Sergeant Stoke this is Chief Inspector Fillimore. Is PC Windsley with you?'

'Yes sir.'

'Where is Windsley now?'

'In the car.'

PC Windsley's voice came over the radio, asking if anyone could hear him. The ashen-faced civilian turned helplessly to the control room sergeant who made a negative signal with a shake of his head.

'I can hear him on the radio now,' Fillimore said. 'Listen Sergeant, there is nothing wrong with your car radio. What I am telling you is for your ears only, you understand me?'

'Yes sir. What's the mystery?' Stoke asked curiously.

'Listen carefully Sergeant.'

Fillimore told Stoke briefly what had happened, and finished by saying, 'Get PC Windsley back here and Sergeant, make it quick.'

The policewoman who had fetched him to the control room handed Fillimore his shoes and socks as he put the phone down. He had forgotten that his feet were bare. He addressed the control room sergeant.

'Bring PC Windsley to my office as soon as he arrives, I'll tell him myself. And keep this to yourselves, we don't want any rumours flying around.'

The information given to Fillimore by the hospital was dreadful. His hand shook as he held the receiver to his ear and heard the news.

Windsley's infant son Steven was dead and his tiny body was so mutilated that the doctor on duty said he would refuse to allow Windsley to see it. His wife Rita was being treated for severe shock. Her injuries were mostly cuts and bruises that could be expected to heal in time but could be expected to leave facial scarring that would require surgery. She had lost a lot of blood.

Fillimore tried not to show his feelings when the control room sergeant knocked on the door and ushered PC Windsley into the office. Windsley looked troubled.

'Sit down PC Windsley. Er, it's David isn't it? I'm sorry David but I have to tell you some very bad news. You remember from your training days that the best way to tell someone is to tell it straight out and not beat about the bush?'

Windsley paled.

'Is it Rita?' he muttered.

Chief Inspector Fillimore told him, as sympathetically as he could. PC Windsley sat with his head in his hands, his body wracked with sobs.

Fillimore spoke again, gently, 'I'll drive you to the hospital myself David, as soon as you feel up to it. I want you to know that I am extremely sorry; very, very sorry, we all are, and if you want any time off you can have all you need. Let me know if there is anything we can do.'

Windsley's lower lip trembled. He drew in a deep breath.

'Yes sir, thank you sir. I'm ready now, I think.'

The hospital smelled of disinfectant and floor polish. A nurse escorted David Windsley to the casualty department, motioning to Fillimore to follow. She peered through a glass-panelled door before she let anyone enter the room. The girl sat up on the casualty bed having one of her heavily bandaged hands treated by a harassed lady doctor wearing a badly creased white coat.

Windsley approached slowly. Rita Windsley stared vacantly at him. Her face was a mess of cuts and scratches and a row of stitches disfigured her left cheek, which was beginning to discolour badly. Both legs were heavily bandaged.

'Rita, Rita, are you all right?'

She seemed not to hear.

'Rita, it's me, David.'

He leaned towards her.

'Rita!'

He looked into the expressionless blue eyes that had once been so beautiful and the awful truth hit him.

'Oh my God! She's...'

The nurse caught him as he slumped down, jarring the bed. The girl who had been Rita Windsley did not notice. With unfocussed eyes she stared at nothing.

***

Stoke briefed the helicopter crew.

'If we see the cat put me down as close as you can, but not too close. Up to a couple of hundred yards I can do the job with the Parker-Hale rifle which fires high velocity semi-jacketed stuff, one shot will be enough. After you've dropped me try and drive the cat towards me if you can. Keep it in sight all the time if you can, and keep an eye on me too, I might need a lift in a hurry!'

The pilot said, 'Can do, but you'll need to be out in the open, say about forty feet from telegraph poles, buildings, trees, and so on.'

Stoke's grin didn't reach his eyes.

'According to Peter Cole, Grimalkin can cover forty feet in one jump. Don't worry, I'm no hero.'

The pilot refrained from comment.

Stoke continued, 'If Grimalkin gets cornered by us or one of the ground patrols I'll go in with the Viking gun, firing special grapeshot. Nasty stuff, you can't get it from you local gunsmith, it's basically nine quarter inch ball bearings in a twelve-bore cartridge. Very nasty. Both barrels of the Viking are choked and special grape at twenty yards should tear the cat in half.'

'At the very least it should make its hide useless for a rug,' the pilot observed, 'but twenty yards is a bit close, don't you think?'

'Too bloody right I do, and if you can think of something better I'm all ears.'

None of the helicopter crew had an answer for him.

'I'm putting PC Croft on board too, he's had the training. Al Croft is Windsley's opposite number on one of the other shifts. Croft will be armed with the semi-automatic rifle which he will use to drive Grimalkin to open ground so that when you drop me off it will be where we want, not where the cat wants. If Croft scores a hit, that's a bonus, but the chances aren't good. What I want from him is rapid fire directed to one side of the cat to make it go the other way. That ought to put the frighteners on it, a rifle bullet going past your ear makes a very loud crack, especially when it's close.'

The pilot wondered how Stoke knew that, and decided not to ask. One of the helicopter crew spoke to PC Croft while Stoke went to make a phone call.

'I wonder what the Chief Constable had to say about his plan for going in close?'

'I expect he'll go along with it when he finds out,' was Croft's astounding reply. 'I wouldn't worry too much about Stoke, he knows how to take care of himself. Don't say I told you or he'll have my scrotum for a tobacco pouch, but he's improperly dressed. If I'd got what he's got I'd wear it on my pyjamas!'

***

Al Croft felt damned uncomfortable and said so as he shifted his backside on the rubber cushion. His unloaded rifle rested across the armrests of his seat and two charged magazines were wedged beside him. Across the cabin Stoke sprawled with the butt of his rifle on the floor. As with Croft, Stoke had two magazines ready for use, though magazines for the Parker-Hale held only four rounds each. The Viking shotgun was within easy reach, Stoke had half a dozen cartridges stuffed into his pockets.

Stoke dozed, and the crewman kept the lookout on his side of the helicopter. Croft was aware that Stoke had hardly slept for several days, he must be all in. Croft kept his own lookout, without real hope of seeing anything through the murkiness of low cloud.

The helicopter flew low, but even so there were wisps of dirty cloud flashing past the windows and the high ground was obscured. The crewman tapped Croft's foot with his boot to gain his attention and held up a bar of chocolate. Croft caught the bar when it was tossed across the cabin, broke off a square and threw it back, and returned to his fruitless vigil. The base of the cloud, the crewman told him, was twelve hundred feet and getting lower. A rainsquall battered the aircraft and made the cabin rattle. Stoke slept on. Another tap from the crewman's boot gained Croft's attention.

The man spoke a few words into his microphone and shouted across the cabin, 'We're going home Al, the driver's had enough. Your man looks knackered and the weather's clagging in fast. I don't reckon we'll be flying tomorrow either.'

The helicopter bounced sickeningly as another gust hammered it and one of Stoke's magazines clattered to the floor. Sergeant Stoke did not stir, he was still asleep when the helicopter grounded fifteen minutes later. PC Croft woke him as the rotors slowed to a stop and he stretched and ran his fingers through his uncombed hair.

'I needed that,' he said.

He looked at his watch.

'That's the longest sleep I've had for days. I suppose you didn't see anything?'

'Couldn't see the ground half the time.'

'Yeah. Thanks for letting me sleep.'

The not unpleasant smell of burnt paraffin from the exhaust filled the cabin when the crewman opened the door. Sergeant Stoke jumped to the ground and Croft passed their weapons to him.

While Croft stowed the rifles into the boot of a waiting car Stoke had a word with the helicopter crew.

'Croft says we won't be flying tomorrow?'

He made the statement a question. The aircraft captain answered him.

'Very unlikely. There's a cold front coming through, that's what's causing this muck, and the latest word is it is speeding up and changing direction. The conditions behind it are good but the next thirty-six hours are expected to be about the same as they are now. The weather people usually get it right. I'll put the crew on stand-by, if there's any chance at all we can be airborne in minutes.'

Sergeant Stoke used the car radio to contact the Mobile Incident Room and spoke to Chief Inspector Fillimore, who had maintained a radio link with the helicopter. Fillimore had heard the weather report that the pilot had received and he instructed Stoke and Croft to return to the police station where he and Superintendent Holley would meet them.

Fillimore was late. PC Al Croft cleaned the rifles and after he had locked them in the armoury Sergeant Stoke initialled his pocketbook and sent him off duty, then settled down to wait. When the chief inspector arrived with Mr Cole he was reading the book he had withdrawn from the library.

'Sorry we're late, there's been a change of plan. The boss has gone to see Ronnie Gleaves again,' Fillimore informed him, 'Mr Cole isn't happy with his account of the shooting incident.'

Cole agreed.

'Quite right. I can't put my finger on it exactly but it doesn't ring true.'

He frowned when he saw what Stoke was reading.

'That's not my best book, you know. I wrote that for the popular market, not the scientific one.'

Stoke chuckled ruefully.

'I know,' he said, 'I saw another one of yours in the reference library. It was too deep for me. I took this one out because of the pictures, I want to see if the cat I saw years ago is in here and try to identify it.'

Mr Cole was interested.

'And?'

'I'm not sure. It was a long time ago. There are some really good pictures in here though. Two I really like.'

'Most people seem to like the leopard on page seventeen. Is that one of your choices?'

'Yes.' Stoke replied, 'and the other is the Scottish Wild Cat. You're the expert, not me, but my guess is that it really was wild when you took that picture. The way it looks right out of the page and it has flattened its ears. I know it's small but it's a tough customer by the look of it.'

'It's tough all right,' Cole said, pushing up his sleeve. 'Look at that. It went for me a second after I took the picture. It was my own fault, I had it cornered with nowhere to run. It would have preferred flight to fight, and when the flash went off in its face I made it really mad and the next thing I knew was that it had its claws in me. I was wearing a thick jersey but it wasn't much protection.'

He seemed proud of the impressive scars the cat had left on his arm.

'Serves me right, I know the rules better than anyone, but it taught me a lesson. It doesn't pay to take any liberties with cats.'

Fillimore leafed through the book rapidly before picking up his note pad.

'Let's get some notes down. Sergeant, how did your end go?' he asked.

'Not too well,' Stoke admitted. 'Most of the time the weather was too murky to see anything. I thought we were on a loser so I got a bit of kip and let PC Croft and the flying crew do the looking. PC Croft came up with a good idea sir, which is worth passing on. He suggested that the technicians put a police radio in Mr Cole's Range Rover and put a number on the roof so we can see it from the air.'

'Good idea!' Fillimore and Cole both exclaimed.

Fillimore made notes.

'I've been taking turns with the boss in the armchair,' Fillimore informed Stoke, 'so we've both had a few minutes sleep. Neither of us reckoned the chances of spotting the cat either. Mr Cole?'

'Agreed. Grimalkin is probably holed up somewhere. Of course I've been wrong in the past,' Cole confessed, 'terribly wrong.'

'Not your fault. Grimalkin is different,' Fillimore consoled him, 'you shouldn't blame yourself for what happened.'

Cole continued to look unhappy. Fillimore scribbled on his pad.

'Sergeant, you keep a shotgun locked away at your place I believe?'

Stoke looked surprised.

'Yes sir, I do a bit of shooting with George Wells now and again,' he replied.

'Good. Take the Viking gun when you go off duty and lock it up with your own gun. Superintendent's orders, just in case we want you in a hurry in the middle of the night. We're moving the Mobile Incident Room by the way. Your girlfriend uses one of her father's fields to fly from, I'm told. George Wells made the offer this afternoon, I think the idea came from her. Level field, access to the road, no obstructions. The flying people gave it the OK, they flew over it this afternoon and took a look.'

Sergeant Stoke was surprised.

'Must've been while I was asleep,' he said, 'I didn't know.'

Stoke and Cole were left alone in the office when Fillimore had finished.

Cole said hesitantly, 'Harry, I still want a chance with my stun gun.'

Stoke nodded.

'You're taking a risk Peter. Not just with Grimalkin, you know about that. I mean with the big chief,' he replied carefully. He shifted awkwardly in his seat. 'I want it dead. I knew Rita Windsley. Know her, I mean. Oh Christ, I've started to say knew already. And her son too. Look Peter, if you want to try that's all right with me, but if I get there first, and I hope I bloody do, I'm not going to play games. If you get there two seconds after me you'll be two seconds too late.'

'I accept that. It's all I can ask for,' Cole said miserably.

***

By the time Superintendent Holley arrived at Ronnie Gleaves' place the rain had ceased, and he had a good look round as he got out of his car. The house stood well back from the yard, and the workshop that bounded one side of the yard was closed. Opposite the workshop Ronnie Gleaves' father was chopping logs and adding them to a pile. When he saw who his visitor was he buried his axe in the chopping block and wiped his hands on his trousers.

'Wotcher mate, ain't seen you for a while. And you didn't have them crowns neither.'

His friendly greeting would have astonished Sergeant Stoke.

'Is it that long? They've been there three years come July. I've come to see young Ronnie. I want a word with him.'

'So do I mate.'

The superintendent lit his pipe and looked astonished when his spent match went straight into the rusty pail he aimed for.

'So do I,' Gleaves repeated. 'I ain't seen him since he got beat up the other night. His mates had a go at him about that there Sid Newcombe, him what was killed. Sniffer had it coming if you ask me. Anyway mate, he tipped a load of waste away in the shed the other day. There's a sump down there, it don't drain straight out, it was a pit for gettin' under vehicles but I covered it up years ago, it ain't in the right place to be any use to me. I dipped it yesterday and what do I find? I'll tell you mate. It ain't the first time. The idle little sod's done it before. There's about three hundred gallons in that sump. Petrol, paraffin, diesel, you name it mate, it's all in there.'

'What are you going to do?'

'Can't leave it. Haven't the gear to pump it out neither. I can rig a low pressure suction pump but it'll take me a day or two to get the stuff together and some drums to pump it into.' He looked up at the scudding clouds. 'Saw your helicopter today mate. You found it yet?'

Superintendent Holley admitted their lack of success. A whining sound came from behind the woodpile and a young puppy appeared. Mr Gleaves picked it up.

'Sniffer's dog. He left her behind when he took off like.'

Remembering something, Holley asked, 'Did he call her Sheba?'

''S'right mate. How did you know?'

'Lucky guess,' Holley chuckled. 'No it wasn't, not really.'

He told the other man how he knew.

'Well I'll be...' Mr Gleaves said. 'Now I come to think of it you're dead right mate. Well I'll be blowed.'

The superintendent felt that the social niceties had gone on long enough.

He said, 'About your Ronnie. He told Sergeant Stoke he shot Grimalkin here. What really happened?'

The man shrugged helplessly.

'Dunno mate, really I don't. It wasn't like he said, ain't nothing ever happens the way he tells it. But I don't know, honest I don't.'

Superintendent Holley believed him, having trouble meeting the man's hurt eyes.

'How are things with you now?' he asked.

Again the shrug of the shoulders.

'I'm all right, sort of. Could do with a bit of help from the lottery, them insurance bills for the workshop is something rotten, but I've got to pay up, haven't I? 'Ere, that sergeant...'

'Sergeant Stoke?'

'Yeah, that's the one. He's all right mate, even if he is a bit hard. Anyway, there was two of them what came. The other one was the kid's father wasn't he? And his misses. Well, you know.'

'That was him. PC Windsley.'

There was a choke in Gleaves' voice as he said, 'I'm sorry mate. I mean they hadn't done nothing had they. It don't seem right. Look mate, if Ronnie comes back I'll give you the wink like. I ain't never shopped anyone but he's got it coming. Long as you don't tell anyone like.'

The superintendent laid a hand on the man's shoulder.

'It's a deal.'

With a hollow feeling he turned away to avoid seeing the tears in Gleaves' eyes.

From behind him he heard a voice call, 'I'll tell my sister I saw you, next time I'm in Bristol.'

***

Sergeant Stoke stood down from his duties the following day. The weather was abysmal, the wind howled across Exmoor, driving curtains of rain in torrents. Overflowing drains poured streams of water into flooded roads and driving conditions were chaotic throughout the county.

Stoke had to make a detour to reach the Wells farm in the afternoon. He dashed through the driving rain to the rear of the house, and Mrs Wells spotted him through the kitchen window and rushed to the door.

'Come in Harry, and take your coat off, you must be soaked,' she greeted him.

Stoke's sodden shoes squelched water as the shrieking gale rattled the windows.

'George is out on the farm somewhere and Jenny is upstairs in her room,' she continued. 'Harry, she's awfully upset, she's been crying all day and she wouldn't come down at lunchtime. I'll make a cup of tea and you can take it up to her. She needs one.'

Which is a lie, she thought. What she needs is you, Harry Stoke, don't let her down now or you'll lose her.

Stoke knocked at the bedroom door. There was no answer. He twisted the doorknob and entered. Jenny lay on her bed with her face buried in her pillow.

'Go away,' came a muffled voice.

Stoke set the cup down.

'I said go away.'

'Jenny, it's me, Harry,' he said softly.

The girl didn't move.

'I don't want to see you. I don't want to see anyone,' she said.

Stoke sat on her bedside chair and stroked her hair.

'I've brought you a cup of tea.'

'I don't want it.'

'Jenny love, it wasn't your fault. It wasn't anybody's fault. You musn't blame yourself for what happened.'

She raised her head and looked at him through swollen eyes.

'He was trying to tell us. He kept saying 'bad pussy' like he did in the shop and I thought he was just playing. Then the cat got him. It was awful Harry, the way he screamed and Rita...'

She broke down with a burst of harsh sobbing.

'I know love, but you couldn't have done anything.'

Suddenly she sat up and threw her arms round him.

'Hold me Harry, hold me please,' she begged.

She laid her face against his chest.

Presently he opened the bedroom window and threw the cold tea out into the storm.

Chapter 9

The Police Mobile Incident Room was parked twenty yards inside the gate of George Wells' field, Jenny's flying field. Parked next to it was a petrol tanker. Superintendent Holley corrected himself, it was a fuel bowser, not a petrol tanker. The flying people had a language of their own. One pilot was named Mike, and so was the crewman, so they were Mike One and Mike Two. Strange people. He approached the helicopter and peered through the perspex window in the pilot's door. A headset lay on each pilot's seat where they had casually dropped them. There were lots of switches and dials. Superintendent Holley did not know the use of any of them.

The Incident Room was stuffy, he had come outside for a breath of fresh air. The weather had changed, it was clear and crisp with no wind and very little cloud. He had noticed a few rotten branches in the road as he drove out of town, and a council crew were shifting a fallen tree that had brought down some power lines. There were reports of flood damage, but nothing serious.

He watched a battered pick-up vehicle pull in through the gate and turn away from the Incident Room. It stopped well away from the helicopter and the superintendent recognised Ronnie Gleaves' father as he climbed out of the vehicle with the alsatian puppy in his arms. Gleaves looked around uncertainly, saw the superintendent, and waved as he started to walk towards him.

'Wotcher mate,' he greeted him.

Superintendent Holley wondered what he wanted and noticed with astonishment that he wore a tie. The knot was clumsy, he wondered when the man had last put a tie on. Never in twenty years as far as he knew.

'I sort of come for a look at the helicopter,' he confided. 'Ain't never seen one close up. It's a nice looking bit of machinery. I like machines.'

Better than you like people, the superintendent thought, and I can't say I blame you. Mr Gleaves held the dog up.

'I give her a new name now, after you told me about how every Alsatian bitch is called Sheba. Her name's Button now.'

Button wriggled and licked the hand that Holley held out. Mr Gleaves found a chocolate drop in his pocket and blew the fluff off it and offered it to the puppy.

'I ain't seen Ronnie,' he said in a low voice.

There was no answer. Superintendent Holley held his peace. Mr Gleaves ran his hand over the metal skin of the helicopter.

'Feel that mate, them flush rivets is as good as I could do myself.'

Superintendent Holley had no idea what a flush rivet was but it was obvious that Mr Gleaves appreciated good engineering.

'I ain't never been in no helicopter mate, and I ain't likely to neither, but do you reckon them back there'd mind if I just looked through the window like?'

He jerked his thumb over his shoulder at the parked vehicles.

'I shouldn't think so, I've just been looking myself.'

The superintendent led the way to the front of the helicopter. In the Incident Room the pilot was talking while Chief Inspector Fillimore and PC Croft monitored the radio.

'Listen in gents, and lady.' Jenny Wells was present. 'I'm flying this morning without Mike One up front with me, he ought to be back about eleven with a new anemometer, ours went bust.'

For the benefit of the non-fliers he explained, 'We've got a hand held anemometer, you walk out into the middle of the field and hold it up and read the wind speed off it. We can live without it, especially this morning with no wind at all to speak of, but we can't rely on good weather for ever. Anyway, we'll do about twenty minutes flying. Our task is two fold. One, to check the radio link and procedures, with Chief Inspector Fillimore as our ground controller. Two, to locate and identify a sample number of marked police vehicles. I forgot about number three, which is to keep an eye out for the cat. Any questions?'

There were none.

The pilot continued.

'Good. It's a straightforward job. One other thing; now we have better weather we'll be flying with the door open. Now I know Miss

Wells is a pilot, by the way I didn't thank you for your tips about local conditions, and I know Sergeant Stoke has already flown with us, but we're going out to the aircraft and Mike Two will run through the drill again. PC Croft, you'll get your brief before your next sortie, after we come down. Ready Mike?'

Mike Two stood up.

'Ready Skipper. This will take about ten or fifteen minutes, then we'll come back in until Chief Inspector Fillimore is ready in about...?'

'Half an hour.'

'Half an hour it is. Chance of a cup of coffee in about fifteen minutes, Al?'

PC Croft gave a thumbs up sign.

Jennifer and Sergeant Stoke led the way to the helicopter. She certainly seemed much better this morning, Stoke thought. Reckon yesterday did us both good.

Jenny was saying the Harry Stoke, 'Daddy got a new dog this morning. Mr North drove over and gave him the choice of two. She's not as nice as the collie, I don't think, but Daddy says she'll do.'

Superintendent Holley and Mr Gleaves did not see them approach, they were on the wrong side of the helicopter. Mr Gleaves lowered his eyes when he saw Jenny and hung back as they walked round the front of the aircraft and he felt everybody's eyes on him.

Plucking up all his courage he said to Stoke, 'Wotcher mate, no hard feelings, you was just doing your job.'

He turned to Jenny, who seemed to him to be an awesome figure in her yellow flying overall.

'You're Miss Wells aren't you Miss. I'm... well it was my boy what shot the cat. I heard about your dog on the news like, and I sort of thought you might like this one. 'Course I didn't know as your dad had already got a dog again. I don't 'spect you want this one now.'

'Thank you, no,' was Jenny's icy reply.

''S'all right Miss, I understand.'

His pleading eyes looked to Superintendent Holley.

'Think I'll go and sit in my car mate. Till you go. I'd like to see it take off, if that's all right.'

Clutching his puppy he broke away and almost ran to his vehicle.

By the time Mike Two had finished his talk about the procedures to be followed Peter Cole had turned up in his Range Rover. When the flying party arrived back in the Mobile Incident Room, which the aircraft crew insisted on calling the caravan, he was telling PC Croft the number that had been put on his roof and the callsign that he had been given, thanking Croft for his suggestion at the same time.

Chief Inspector Fillimore looked up from the radio.

'Nearly ready sir,' he informed Superintendent Holley. 'I've got five more rifles on the way. Rogers, Ayers, and Smith, from our neighbours in Bath, and Sergeant Mann and PC Woolly from Bristol. They have their own cars and I've allocated callsigns to them, but I haven't got their roof numbers yet.'

He continued, 'When they get here I'll split them up and put each marksman with a local man who knows the area, so that will probably mean new callsigns. I'll keep you informed.'

'Well done Jock.'

Holley accepted a coffee from PC Croft and balanced it precariously on a window ledge while he filled his pipe.

'Five more guns,' Peter Cole said. 'If only I knew more. I keep blaming myself for...'

Superintendent Holley rounded on him and Jenny.

'Shut up,' he hissed through clenched teeth. 'I've had enough from the pair of you. It's all my fault, that's all I ever hear. Well it isn't. It's not anyone's fault. You see that poor bastard out there,' he jabbed his pipe in the direction of the pick-up vehicle, 'that's Ronnie Gleaves' father. His son shot the cat. Not him, his son, and now he's got the whole world dumping on him. How do you think he feels,' Holley roared, 'he came here this morning to see if there was anything he could do, any little thing. And what happens? I'll tell you what happens. He offered his dog. He was just trying to make amends for something he didn't even do, that's all it was. That was his widow's mite, all he had to give. And you treated him like shit. All right, you didn't know, but that's not the point, you didn't bloody care. Look at him now. Have you ever seen a rabbit in your headlights? Too scared to run and he can't fight back because he hasn't anything to fight with, that's what he is, just a rabbit. And all you can do, both of you, is keep saying it's your fault about Windsley's kid and... and you make me sick, the bloody pair of you!'

Jenny's chin turned white and quivered.

'I didn't think...' she started to say, and broke off, biting her lip.

'Of course it's not his fault,' Cole muttered thickly. 'I'll go and tell him.'

'Wait for me,' Jenny gulped, and bolted for the door.

Holley glared at Stoke.

'Well mister. Have you got something to say?' he demanded.

In the hush that followed Stoke rose to his feet.

'I've got plenty to say.'

There was a dramatic pause.

'Thanks for the lesson in how to handle her. It might come in handy some day.'

The superintendent's face creased in a huge grin.

'Well you old bastard,' he boomed, 'she's got you, eh? She's a damn fine girl.'

He pumped Stoke's hand.

Five minutes later Chief Inspector Fillimore looked up from his desk.

'Ready when you are,' he told the pilot.

'OK, let's go. Mike, shout Miss Wells, will you, we don't want to leave her behind.'

Mike Two attracted Jenny's attention by waving his hand and pointing at he helicopter, which she reached before the crew. At the entrance door the pilot paused.

'Silly of me. I forgot Mike One isn't with us. Miss Wells, would you like to fly at the sharp end?'

'Oh yes,' Jenny was pleased. 'I'd love to.'

Then her face set in a stubborn look.

'No I wouldn't,' she said. 'Let Mr Gleaves have it.'

'Jenny,' Sergeant Stoke protested.

She stamped her foot.

'Don't Jenny me, Harry Stoke. If Mr Gleaves doesn't go I'm not going either and that's final.'

Superintendent Holley cleared his throat.

'It's a bit irregular,' he said.

Jenny got a bit of her own back.

'It's a bit irregular for me to go too, isn't it?' she stormed, 'So what's the difference? There's a spare seat and I want him to have it. Now who's treating him like...' she stopped and turned scarlet.

Mike Two looked at his captain.

'Skipper?'

'OK by me.'

'And OK by me,' Holley growled.

Jenny bounded off to fetch Mr Gleaves.

'She's found me out.' Superintendent Holley moaned with a huge grin on his face.

Seconds later Jenny thrust a wriggling puppy at him.

'Hold Button,' she said, and disappeared into the fuselage while Mr Gleaves was being urged towards the cockpit, wiping his eye on his sleeve, ''cos I've got something in it mate.'

Mike Two and Harry Stoke sat on opposite sides of the open door and Jenny occupied the far side of the cabin. The pilot started the engine and the smell of the exhaust suddenly reminded Jenny of the days when she flew as an airline stewardess.

The helicopter rocked as the pilot increased the revolutions and then the ground was falling away rapidly.

Jenny unhooked the spare headset from the bulkhead behind her seat, glanced at Mike Two and pointed to her ear. Mike Two nodded affirmative so she put it on. She heard Chief Inspector Fillimore directing them to a location where a police vehicle was supposed to be, and soon she was able to see the number on the roof of the car. Harry Stoke consulted a checklist to confirm the identities of the occupants and whether a marksman was in the car, then spoke briefly to them and counted one to five.

'Loud and clear,' a voice crackled in her ear.

She soon became bored with the radio chatter which was a series of tests which were nothing new to her, so she took off the headset and settled down to enjoy the view. Her experienced eye informed her that they were flying at about five hundred feet above the ground and she watched the familiar scene with pleasure. Several times she spotted police vehicles and saw Harry Stoke mouth something into his microphone. They turned towards home and Mike Two leaned across the cabin and tapped her knee and pointed to the headphones she had taken off. She wondered what he and Harry were laughing about. The helicopter rocked as she put the phones over her ears. She soon found out why.

'OK, that was pretty good, better than my first try. Now try a turn to starboard, keep your head up, don't look at the instruments, just aim for the big tree on top of the hill. That's it, lean the stick, you don't need any rudder. OK, fine, straighten up, good, good, steady. Well done.'

'Was that right what I did?'

'Right on the button. OK, we're about a mile from the field. I'm starting my descent. Follow me through, that's fine, you've got a nice touch. Field coming up, there's the caravan dead ahead. Fine, levelling at two fifty feet, speed now twenty knots and there we are, right on top of it. Good, now I want a right turn so I can have a good look at the field before we land, no forward speed so we'll give it a bit of rudder, straighten her up, keep following me through on the controls, lever down just a fraction, feel it, little bit more and...'

Jenny grinned with delight at Harry and Mike Two. As soon as the rotor stopped she was unstrapped and she jumped out when Mike gave the all clear, and raced at assist the beaming Mr Gleaves from the cockpit while he thanked the pilot.

'That was all right mate, I ain't never done nothing like that before. Don't 'spect my sister in Bristol will believe it when I tell her. All right Miss, I'm coming. Thanks again mate.'

'Stop calling me Miss, Mr Gleaves. I'm Jenny to you. What's your name?'

'Brian Miss. Jenny,' he said shyly.

'Come on Brian, let's go and fetch Button, shall we?'

Jenny led him by the arm.

Mike Two nudged Sergeant Stoke.

'Some girl,' he commented. 'I've heard of her before, you know.'

Stoke raised an interrogative eyebrow.

'How come?' he enquired.

'Word gets around the flying clubs. A guy in Wales who flies micros told me a couple of months ago about a girl on Exmoor who flies a yellow wing. He didn't know her name or her club, but he'd heard she was good. She's got her AFI hasn't she?'

'What's that?'

'Sorry,' Mike apologised. 'Assistant Flying Instructor.'

'Oh. Should have guessed. Yes, she is an instructor. Is she as good as she says she is?' Stoke asked curiously.

Mike grinned again.

'The bloke in Wales says she's the best, he's heard,' he replied.

Inside the Incident Room PC Croft served Mr Gleaves with a cup of coffee.

'Blimey Sarge, I never thought I'd see the day,' he whispered to Stoke.

'Neither did he. Shut up,' Stoke shot back at him. 'There are a lot of things that will never be the same since Sniffer shot that bloody cat.'

Croft gloomily agreed.

Brian Gleaves approached Superintendent Holley. He was still jaunty after being allowed to handle the controls of the helicopter, but diffident about offering a suggestion. Holley gave him a sympathetic hearing. Mr Gleaves shuffled his feet.

'Well it's like this mate. I reckon animals is a bit like people. What I mean is I seen the animals today, cows an' sheep and all, and they all looked up at me. I did the other day when I saw the helicopter but I don't no more when Miss Wells, Jenny, flies her aeroplane around, and nor don't the animals I reckon, an' I mean the cat too. Grimalkin.'

He spat the hated name.

'We're used to it, see, an' it seems to me that the way to find the cat is with the little yellow aeroplane mate, not the helicopter.'

The superintendent gaped and grasped his arm.

'Do you know,' he said, 'I really think you might have something.'

Jenny approached.

'We'd better go Brian,' she said, 'the policemen have a lot of work to do. Will you drive me home? It's only across the field and I'll hold Button for you.'

Jenny could have walked the distance in ten minutes, the way she had arrived, but she wanted to do all she could to make up for her earlier bad manners. Besides, Harry had been angry with her for walking, and she knew he was right. There was no telling where Grimalkin would strike again.

Mr Gleaves was still talking about his flight.

'Did you enjoy it?' Jenny asked him.

'It was great Miss. Jenny I mean. Is it always like that? I mean, your little yellow one is different, isn't it?'

'Would you like to see it?' Jenny asked impulsively. 'Come on Brian, it won't take long. I'm not flying while the helicopter is here but we can look at it. Would you like to?'

Mr Gleaves astonished Jenny with his knowledge of engineering. He examined the machine and tested the rigging, and checked the locknuts for safety.

'Have to show one and a half clear threads they do, and you shouldn't be able to turn them with your fingers. Yours are all right. That's a neat little engine.'

Jenny soon realised that her aircraft was receiving a very thorough inspection. Brian asked a question hesitantly.

'Who looks after these at your club? I mean, I know you have to have licences and things, but I had papers once and I was sort of wondering...'

He looked at her hopefully. Jenny saw her chance. She would have liked to apologise to him before, but she knew he would be embarrassed and she had done enough harm already.

'I'll find out for you.' She promised. 'Brian, would you like to come flying with me? I'll fly down to the club and you can talk to the CFI about it. If you want to.'

She felt almost shy about asking him. Mr Gleaves was almost overcome. He had no idea what a CFI was but he did know engineering. 'Course he mustn't get any big ideas but...

***

Mr William Newton, who's spelling was an accurate reflection of his personality, was apprehended in the act of decorating a bus shelter with an aerosol spray. 'Grimalkine kils the Filth,' he wrote, and 'Grimalkine ruls OK.' He made his court appearance the following morning with his arm in a sling.

His companion Mary Tait was well known for her bizarre conduct. She went berserk and was charged with causing grievous bodily harm to Newton by breaking his arm, and causing actual bodily harm to Constable Moore, Policewoman Croft, and Policewoman Sergeant Miller. Other charges included criminal damage to the bus shelter, a police vehicle, and a cell at the police station.

Newton paid his fine. Tait was remanded for psychiatric reports.

Simon Hart was less fortunate. The letter that he had addressed to the Chief Constable was produced in court. It read, 'Grimalkin 3, Police 0. You can't catch me. Ha Ha.'

Hart had bragged to his workmates and showed signs that rough justice had already been administered. His picture appeared on the front page of his local paper, and hours later Hart begged for police protection.

Chapter 10

Stoke and PC Croft flew a regular patrol at first light and another in the afternoon. Nothing of Grimalkin was seen and Superintendent Holley talked to the helicopter crew about using Jenny's microlight as a spotter aircraft. Mike One, the co-pilot agreed that in principle the idea was worth trying but he pointed out that Jenny was restricted as to what she was permitted to do.

'She can take Harry Stoke up with her, the way she's been doing,' he explained, 'but not with his gun. I assume you had something like that in mind?'

Holley admitted that he had.

'Thought so. Well I know that aviation law is a closed book to most policemen, so I'll put you in the picture. First, no weapons may be carried. Our crew has got special dispensation to have firearms on board because we've worked with the police before, but Jenny would lose her licence if she even thought about it. Second, and I'm none too sure about this myself, Jenny may have operational restrictions. I'm not familiar with the rules for microlights, except in a general way. She flies under Visual Flight Rules, and a VFR pilot is grounded in claggy weather, or even good weather if there is ground haze. And she's not commercial, she'd be doing it for free, except I believe you're allowed to pay for her fuel. And you can be dead sure she'd have to carry extra insurance.'

The superintendent thought about it.

'I want that aircraft, I really do. I think Brian Gleaves was right about the cat. Can she get exemptions?'

'Not for the safety rules, no way. I think the rest could be sorted out but I'd hate to have to pay the bill.'

Holley grunted.

'That's my pigeon, leave it to me.'

'You're the boss. Mind if I make a suggestion?'

Filling his pipe, Holley replied, 'I'm listening.'

'Well it's like this,' Mike One explained. 'Microlighters are a bit touchy about breaking the rules. I'll give you a bit of background. The sport started to take off, no pun intended, a few years ago when hang gliding started. It wasn't long before some bright sparks started putting engines on them, there was no law against it. They started killing themselves and microlights got a bad press as a consequence. Some aircraft designs were a bit dodgy too. There were calls for microlight aircraft to be banned, which was stupid because it would have driven the sport underground, but a bunch of pilots made a nuisance of themselves with the CAA and now they have their own representative body, answerable to the Civil Aviation Authority but with a fair bit of clout.'

The superintendent's spent match missed the bin and he said, 'Go on.'

'Well, the microlight outfit represents its pilot's interests, but they have a duty to keep their members in line, and they don't pull their punches, they come down like a ton of bricks for any breach of the regulations. They had to fight so long and hard for recognition that they really clamp down.'

'Hmm. So there's no chance of getting Jenny's aircraft then? Suppose you were to fly it?'

'Christ I couldn't fly that! Neither could the skipper, we're both NFQ. Uh, not qualified.'

'I see,' Holley said. 'I must remember that expression. So I'm stuck then?'

The pilot shook his head.

'I didn't say that. I know someone in Jenny's organisation as it happens, and I can put you in touch with him. I guarantee he'll move heaven and earth to help. If there is a way, he'll find it.'

'I appreciate it.' The superintendent blew a cloud of smoke. 'I'll get her agreement first of course, I wouldn't dream of going behind her back.'

'She stood up to you all right,' the pilot reminded him.

Holley beamed.

'Didn't she though! She was a bloody marvel.' He thought for a moment. 'What you said about her machine. Could you fly it?'

'Nope. I've never handled a micro. Have you seen it?'

'I missed her this morning when she flew off somewhere but I've seen it from my garden once or twice. She looks as if she's sitting in a yellow pea pod.'

Mike One laughed.

'Good description. That design didn't happen overnight. Jenny's aircraft is as technically advanced as our helicopter is. More advanced in some ways. In the early days they were all noise and no go, but now they are quieter and they shove out power like nobody's business, and some of the materials used in Jenny's aircraft weren't even thought of when the helicopter came off the drawing boards. Mike the crewman could tell you more about that, he has to know a hell of a lot of engineering in his job.'

'I'm impressed,' Holley admitted.

'You should be. I don't know what her performance profile is but I'm pretty sure her speed would make your hair stand on end if she really bent the throttle. As far as height is concerned, well, I don't know.'

'Sergeant Stoke told me she climbed to several thousand feet the other day,' the superintendent said.

'Micros aren't toys, they're as real as jumbo jets.' The pilot stood up and walked around the room. 'They're a lot better than you know,' he continued, 'Jenny doesn't need all that field to take off and land. Even with a full fuel tank and two on board she can be off the ground in a few yards and she can land just about anywhere I can. She could drop Harry Stoke and get clear in a couple of seconds and if she's half as good as I hear she is she could drive the cat in any direction you want, the same as I can.'

Holley looked surprised.

'I was thinking more of getting a shot at it from the air,' he said.

'Uh huh, no way. It might work in the movies, but not for real.'

The pilot gazed out of the window and continued, 'I don't like it, you'll be asking her to take a hell of a risk.'

Holley agreed.

Standing up, he confessed. 'I don't like it much either. I think she'll go for it because Rita Windsley was her friend from their schooldays and they flew for the same airline. They were pretty close. I hate to ask her, that's the worst part of my job, sitting behind a desk and sending other people to do the dirty work. But what choice have I got?' he demanded angrily, 'her aircraft is one of my best hopes. I must ask her, don't you understand, I must!'

He banged his fist on the window ledge in fury. Both men stared out of the window.

***

Despite what she had told Brian Gleaves, Jenny Wells did fly her aircraft while the helicopter was using her field. Her Chief Flying Instructor telephoned her and she agreed to fly to see him in the morning. He promised her a sandwich lunch, provided she brought her own sandwiches, and rung off. Remembering her promise to Brian Gleaves she tried to contact him, but after getting the unobtainable tone she drove to his yard and found him building a kennel and an enclosed pound for Button the dog. She held the wire netting against a post while he banged staples into the wood.

'Thanks Miss,' he said as he drove the last one home.

'Jenny,' she reminded him. 'All my friends call me Jenny.'

He glowed with pleasure.

She told him about the call from her flying club and that she was going to fly after all, and asked him if he could take the day off to fly with her. The look on his face gave her his answer before he opened his mouth.

'That'd be grand. I was going to start pumping the waste from the workshop tomorrow but I ain't got enough drums anyway. There's a sump under the floor what was made to stand in and work underneath motors but I covered it over because it ain't no use, and now it's full of waste oil and such. Can't leave it, or the whole place could go up. What should I wear?' he asked anxiously.

'Well, you'd be lost in Harry's flying clothes. Better just wear something warm.'

'Right ho. He is a big 'un, isn't he? Taller'n you even. I can't match him, 'cepting round the middle maybe.'

Brian grinned and patted his stomach.

'Has your son come home yet?' Jenny asked hesitantly.

Brian laid down his hammer and scratched his head.

'He ain't showed up yet. Funny thing is Jenny, I know I shouldn't say it but I don't want him to. He ain't been nothing but trouble to me all his life an' every day I sort of wake up and hope he ain't coming back today. He's my son but he's a wrong 'un. I got this sort of feeling he's gone for good this time and I ain't sorry. I just ain't and that's all there is to it.'

***

Brian arrived early for his flight. Jenny strapped him into the tiny cockpit and made sure that his helmet and goggles were on properly. The engine ran smoothly as she applied power and released the brakes. Within seconds they were airborne. Maintaining a steady climb she altered course at five hundred feet and eased the throttle, and settled down to fly to her flying club.

The crowd of police officers who had gathered to watch the departure dispersed to their duties.

'She didn't even wave,' PC Croft complained.

The take off had been an anticlimax.

The helicopter captain directed his answer to everybody.

'I said she was reckoned to be good. I wouldn't care to fly with a pilot who plays to the crowd. Jenny is very professional.'

Sergeant Stoke said, 'I marked her take off run. I'm going over there top pace it out.'

'It was short,' the pilot agreed, 'but I wouldn't bother. If she was really grabbing for air she would have been off in half the distance. She had two on board as well, but if she was on her own and in a real hurry she'd have stood on her tail as soon as she was off the ground and gone up like an angel going home. I tell you, Jenny could fly off a tennis court.'

***

While Brian Gleaves was being shown around the flying club Jenny was talking to the Chief Flying Instructor.

'I've booked the Cessna for half an hour. If I'd known your stuff would be here today I'd have booked a full hour. The right hand seat's yours if you want it.'

Jenny declined the offer.

'I'll sit in the back. Ask Brian if he would like a trip, I think he would like that. He'd never had his backside off the ground until yesterday and now he's had all of forty minutes flying time.'

'Any friend of yours. He'll have to become a temporary member and pay for a familiarisation flight.'

'Pretty please.'

'OK, no fee. Don't tell the club secretary.'

Jenny's flying club was not much to look at. A businessman who owned his own aircraft had rented the club a corner of his field and the premises were little more than a couple of shacks that housed the aircraft. There was a small workbench. Brian Gleaves examined everything carefully, then walked outside and strolled respectfully round the Cessna aircraft.

Jenny saw him through the window and told her CFI why she had brought him with her. She talked at some length, until a mechanic interrupted to say that their take off time was near. He also informed the astonished pair that the unidentified piece of machinery that had lain under the bench for as long as anyone could remember was a Brunton Swager. Apparently Brian Gleaves had told him what it was for and claimed that he could repair it in a couple of hours. Jenny told them how he had examined her microlight the previous day. You wouldn't think it to look at him, Jenny mused, but Brian Gleaves was a first class engineer. The CFI removed a flying overall from his locker.

'He's about my size,' he said, 'give him a shout.'

For the third time it two days Brian Gleaves found himself looking down on the landscape below, and this time he was quite high, much higher than he had been in the helicopter or with Jenny in her little aeroplane. He could even see a small cloud beneath him. Six thousand feet, he had been told.

He studied the instruments. The fuel and temperature gauges were easy enough, and so were the pressures. The flying instruments were unfamiliar but he soon found the one he wanted and worked it out. If he'd got it right the reading was six thousand two hundred feet. He liked to be accurate about things like that, after all, that's what instruments were for.

The CFI's voice sounded in his ear. He had to ask for the question to be repeated. The pilot asked him how he was enjoying the flight. Brian told him he thought it was fine, and asked about the height. The pilot looked surprised and admitted that he was flying two hundred feet higher than the figure he had given Brian.

He swivelled his head to look at Jenny and made a circle with his thumb and forefinger. Brian was OK.

Back on the ground the CFI asked him if Jenny had been giving him flying lessons.

Jenny answered the question.

'Certainly not. I only own half the Red Arrow, the bank owns the other half. If Brian wants lessons he'll pay like anyone else.'

What she said was true, but the real reason was that Jenny had learned not to be patronising, even if she had been made to learn the hard way. She had grown up a bit since meeting Brian Gleaves, she reflected. And since the superintendent had yelled at her.

With some difficulty Brian was persuaded that the flying overall he was wearing was an old one that the CFI had not got round to throwing away, and he was to keep it for the flight back with Jenny.

'All right mate,' he said at last, 'but them wings has got to come off. I ain't pretending to be something I'm not.'

Jenny left them talking while she went to inspect the work being done on her aircraft.

When the time came for them to depart Jenny used the club phone to talk to Chief Inspector Fillimore and give him her estimated time of arrival, and asked if the helicopter was operating in the area she would be using. Fillimore informed her that the afternoon patrol had just landed and would not be airborne again unless Grimalkin was sighted, but he would inform the aircraft captain that she was on her way back, just in case. He then asked Jenny to do something that he said was important and would explain later. He left Jenny feeling very puzzled.

Jenny handed Brian a different helmet for the return flight and showed him what had been done to her aircraft.

'We can talk to each other much better now,' she told him. 'I would have had it done before but there was every colour of helmet in stock except yellow, and I've made yellow my colour and I wouldn't take anything else.'

She told Brian what the chief inspector had asked her to do.

'I won't do it if you don't want to,' Jenny said, 'it might not be very nice.'

Brian Gleaves admitted that he was apprehensive but expressed his willingness to co-operate.

During the flight he mused on his change of fortune. He had come to realise that after his wife had left him he had become something of a recluse. Now he had suddenly made new friends and he was sorting out a few ideas in his mind, and Ronnie had gone. For good, he hoped.

Brian had not told the superintendent that Ronnie had sneaked into the house and stolen some money before he vanished. He had got away with sixty pounds and some loose change, all there was in the house. It was a small price to pay to be rid of him, he had discharged his duties to Ronnie a long time ago and if he'd got any sense he'd have kicked him out years ago. It was a good thing Ronnie had not known about his bank money, not that he could have got his thieving hands on it if he had.

For twenty years Brian Gleaves had spent one night in every four weeks with his sister in Bristol. Every time he took some money with him, and his sister showed him his deposit book with the last payment recorded. The sums were not large, sometimes only a couple of pounds in the early years, but with time, and what with the interest, he had managed to get a nice little nest egg together. Perhaps he ought to have got out a bit more and spent some of it, but it was no use crying over spilt milk. His reverie was broken by Jenny's voice in his helmet.

'We're getting close Brian. Check your straps.'

He did so and acknowledged her order. The airfield slid towards them.

'There it is,' Brian reported.

There were a lot more vehicles on the ground now than when they had left.

'Hang on!'

The spectators saw the low flying aircraft suddenly enter a steep dive, aiming straight at the ground.

'She's going to crash!' Some body shouted and began running towards the point of impact. At the very last moment the aircraft levelled out and hit the ground, jerking to a savage stop as Jenny put the brakes full on. She held the aircraft for fifteen seconds while the engine ran up to full power, all the time glaring with compressed lips at the camera crew who were obviously filming her. She released the brakes and almost at once the aircraft lifted clear of the ground. Jenny pointed the nose skyward and held the Red Arrow in a steep climb. She levelled and began a curving dive, still under full power, straight at the camera. At head height she screamed towards it, lifted slightly and went into a tight turn, the yellow wing scorching past the camera crew, some of whom flung themselves flat on the ground.

Jenny performed a tight circuit and landed again, this time more gently, and taxied to the Mobile Incident Room.

'I was too scared to look and too scared not to,' gasped Brian.

Jenny replied through tight lips.

'I didn't plan that last bit until I saw that camera,' she confessed. 'I thought if they want pictures I'll give them some they won't forget in a hurry. It was a damn stupid thing to do.'

A crowd of police officers surrounded the aircraft.

PC Croft said, 'Half of us down here thought you were going to crash.'

'Half of us up there thought so to mate,' was the shaken reply.

Jenny shook her hair free of her helmet and fixed Superintendent Holley with an angry glare.

'Now perhaps you'll tell me what this is all about!' she snapped.

***

Harry Stoke exploded in fury when the plan was put to him.

Red faced with anger he raged, 'You can't ask Jenny to do that! Grimalkin's bloody dangerous and if anything goes wrong it's her life at risk. I won't let her have anything to do with a crackpot scheme like that!'

'Shall we wait and see what she says?' Superintendent Holley said mildly.

Jenny was less than amused when he explained that he had wanted to see if she could land and take off again from a confined space with a passenger.

'You could have asked me and I would have told you!' she stormed. 'It wasn't fair on Mr Gleaves!'

'We, that is, I, needed to know if it was possible with an inexperienced passenger,' he explained, and told her what he was asking her to do.

'Well next time you want me to do anything like that I'm putting you in the passenger seat!' Jenny raged, and was defeated by the superintendent's grin of acceptance.

Brushing Harry Stoke's protests aside she agreed but reminded him that she could only land on short grass, unlike the helicopter that could land on heather. Also, she needed flat ground. That left plenty of places where she could operate safely. However, unless she received official clearance she would have nothing to do with it.

Brian Gleaves helped her put the Red Arrow in Jenny's hangar and insisted on giving it a thorough inspection before he drove off. Jennifer changed out of her flying clothing and went to visit Rita and David in hospital.

David Windsley was sitting up in bed. He was pale and obviously sedated, listless when spoken to and answering questions but not volunteering information or asking questions of his own.

As Jenny left he suddenly said, 'It was all Sniffer Gleaves' fault,' and lapsed into silence.

Rita Windsley was on an upper floor and she looked ghastly. Her bruises had developed into massive discolorations and the stitches in her face pulled her mouth to one side. Jennifer had always considered her to be beautiful rather than merely pretty, but her looks were gone for good. The worst thing, Jenny thought, were her eyes. They were dull and unseeing as Rita stared blindly at her. Jennifer's own eyes filled with tears as she sat by Rita's bed and tried to talk to her. There was no sign from Rita that she knew she was there.

'Can she see us?' she whispered to the nurse who had accompanied her.

'Her pupils respond normally but the message isn't getting through. She can hear as well but she doesn't understand anything. There is treatment and with time, but...' the nurse stopped talking.

Jenny's eyes asked the question that she dared not put into words. The nurse shook her head.

'I shouldn't tell you this really, but they don't think she'll ever recover.'

The tone was sympathetic but the words were brutal. Jenny left the hospital in tears and cried all the way home.

There was no one in the side ward on the ground floor to hear David Windsley repeat out loud, 'It was all Sniffer Gleaves' fault.'

Well it was, wasn't it? He was the one who shot Grimalkin and Sergeant Stoke had told Sniffer he would have a lot to answer for because of it. His son Steven was dead and they wouldn't let him see him, and Rita was in the same hospital and would never leave it, except to go to a home for people like her. They hadn't told him when they let him see her, but he knew. All they could say was how wonderful the modern treatments were, as if he was someone off the streets and not a policeman. Well, he knew a lie when he heard one, even if they thought they were doing him a favour.

At his home, Brian Gleaves put Button in her kennel for the night, after cleaning and filling her water bowl. He had stopped on his way home and bought a rubber bone and a chewing strip. Brian shut the gate carefully and went indoors.

He made himself something to eat, not much, just beans on toast, and settled down to do some figuring. He had talked to the mechanic at the flying club and he was beginning to put some ideas together. When he turned on the television to watch the news he saw the piece of film that the camera crew had taken when he and Jenny had arrived back at the flying field that afternoon and he held his breath as the yellow aircraft dived towards the ground and levelled out just in time. The picture changed and the aircraft shot towards the camera and banked so that the wing flashed past only inches away. Blimey, it looked worse on the ground than it did in the air, and that was saying something!

Brian had not realised that filming was still taking place as he and Jenny got out of the aircraft.

'Pilot Jenny Wells and her observer Brian Gleaves are taking part in the search for Grimalkin,' the newsreader said.

Brian sighed with relief when the item ended and there had been no mention of the fact that his son had been the one who shot the cat, and then he had another thought. He hoped his sister in Bristol was watching the news. She'd have to believe him when he told her about it now. Couldn't argue with them pictures, could she!

***

Grimalkin skirted the field where there was police activity, darted across the road, and used a shallow ditch for cover as it left the Wells farm. The ditch was filled with cold water but the cat did not mind and only its head showed as it made its way against the weak current. The cold water soothed the cat's aching paw and helped reduce the swelling. The wound was healing nicely although it would be some time before the cat could put any weight on it.

When the helicopter passed overhead Grimalkin was still in the water, invisible and shielded by the grass that grew along the banks.

Clear of the cultivated land, the cat used the tough springy heather for cover as it made its way uphill towards the high ground. Once again the helicopter passed over and it froze on its belly until the danger was past, then it began its purposeful journey again. At midday it rested and the warm sun felt good on its dark flanks as it licked the broken paw.

Towards nightfall Grimalkin changed direction and made for a small copse where it killed and ate an unwary game bird, then settled down to sleep.

Chapter 11

Constable Rogers, one of the marksmen on loan from Bath, finished the remaining crumbs of his pasty and washed it down with the last of his half pint of lager. The civilian sports jacket worn over his uniform did nothing to disguise his profession. PC Rogers and Mr Cole had endured the curiosity of the landlord who served them, and parried his questions.

Rogers remarked as he found a corner table, 'You have to be careful sometimes. A casual word has been know to turn into 'a police spokesman said,' all over the front page. It can make life bloody.'

Peter Cole re-read the type written statement prepared by a witness who claimed to have seen the cat at close quarters.

'I suppose you know he was lying,' PC Rogers interrupted his train of thought.

Mr Cole pencilled a short note at the foot of the page and signalled agreement with a slight inclination of his head.

'It's a fair description of a big cat, I'll grant you, but it came straight out of his head,' Rogers continued.

Peter Cole looked amused.

'Actually,' he replied, 'this is a very good description of a lynx, and I ought to know.'

He paused briefly and enjoyed the expression on the PC's face.

'I ought to know,' he repeated, 'because he copied this word for word from a book I wrote myself. I'm not sure how I feel about that, flattered that he bought my book, or annoyed that he though he could get away with it.'

'I should feel flattered. He couldn't have known you were going to pitch up on his doorstep. I'd like to be there when he catches on,' Rogers replied.

They were eating a pub lunch at a place that Superintendent Holley had recommended to Peter Cole. They had called on three people who claimed to have seen the cat. The first had been an ancient and mildly cantankerous old lady who telephoned to say she had taken a picture of Grimalkin years previously. She produced it triumphantly.

'That's my great granddaughter when she was three years old and there's the cat in the background. I only take black and white pictures because I'm quite colour blind. There was nobody else there when I took the picture, good heavens no! But when I got the film back from the chemist there was the cat staring right at me.'

Constable Rogers examined the picture, shaking his head doubtfully as he passed it to Mr Cole.

'You can't see it, can you,' the old woman exclaimed. 'Neither can anyone else except my eldest granddaughter, she's colour blind like me and she can see it. She'll tell you it's there all right.'

Mr Cole pursed his lips as he studied the photograph.

'Just you remember who's picture that is, young fellow,' the old woman said, 'if anyone sells it to the papers it'll be me. You just take it and show it to one of those computer things and it will tell you where to look. But it's my picture, remember.'

Mr Cole promised to return the photograph to her personally at her house near Ash Mill, close to where the cat had first been reported some years previously.

'How did you know that chap wasn't telling the truth?' he asked PC Rogers, returning to the subject of the written statement, which he still held. 'Years of experience I suppose?'

PC Rogers gave an eloquent shrug.

'Not on your life,' he denied, 'I knew as soon as I saw him, before he opened his mouth. It was pure prejudice and nothing else. It's a long story but I'll try and keep it short. When I was a lad I lived in a back street terrace in Bath, my parents still live there. Anyway, there was a woman a few doors down the street from us, called Mrs Shore, not that it matters. Mrs Shore's grandfather served in the navy once, Merchant Navy I believe, not Royal, it must've been way back in the days of sail, and I remember her saying that only a seafaring man ought to wear a beard and it should be a proper beard at that. She couldn't abide variations on a theme, according to Mrs Shore it's a sure sign that the wearer can't be trusted, so when I saw matey's goatee beard, what Mrs Shore would have called hair-round-his-mouth, I started listening for a lie. It's damn silly but you'd be surprised how often I've found the old biddy knew what she was talking about.'

Peter Cole pulled a face.

'And I thought it was something special.'

'Isn't it special?' Rogers argued. 'Mrs Shore has been around long enough to have developed a sort if instinct, she must be getting on for eighty. I'm not saying that all bearded non-sailors are crooked but whenever I deal with anyone like our friend back there I always expect the worst, but don't tell that to the Sunday papers.'

Mr Cole returned the statement to Constable Rogers, who placed it in a plain file, and they left the inn.

The policeman drove while Mr Cole sat in the passenger seat and considered the facts as he knew them.

The cat appeared to favour low ground, but since the shooting it had retreated to the higher places in the Exmoor National Park. Cole wondered why. There was still something about Sniffer Gleaves' account of events that left a small niggle in the back of his mind. He wished he could put his finger on it. Constable Rogers asked a question.

'Why did he describe a lynx? You said that you think Grimalkin is a leopard.'

Cole yawned. He had nearly fallen asleep.

Shaking himself awake he replied. 'I did and I do, but it's been called a lynx before, although it's never been properly identified. I'll know for sure when I see it myself.'

'Well sir, I hope I see it before you do. I don't fancy your job one bit. It's one thing for me or the other marksmen to have a go at long range with a rifle, but your dart gun is a bit too short range for my liking. You've got to get it first time, and what happens if you miss?'

Peter Cole's tone was deceptively light as he replied, 'If I miss with my first shot I'll try to look as if I'm somewhere else and hope like hell it runs away!'

Out of the corner of his eye Constable Rogers noticed Cole's knuckles whiten as he spoke. Rogers had come very close to asking the question which Cole had been consciously avoiding since becoming involved in the Grimalkin affair. His gun was a very short-range weapon, and it was all too true that he must make his first shot count. Grimalkin was not likely to give second chances. What Cole had carefully omitted to tell anyone was that an animal as big as he estimated Grimalkin to be was not simply going to lie down and go to sleep. As a scientist Peter Cole was determined to capture the animal alive if he could. As a human being he was very much aware that he might have to run for his life before the drug took effect, and if his sums were wrong he stood a very good chance of losing the race.

He cursed Ronnie 'Sniffer' Gleaves for the foul shot that had injured the cat.

Constable Rogers allowed a few minutes to pass before he mentioned Grimalkin again.

'I read in the paper that the cat's had two thousand sheep. That's two hundred a year for ten years. Seems like a hell of a lot of sheep to me.'

He looked expectantly at Mr Cole, waiting for a reply.

'One every three or four days,' Cole replied eventually. I've been thinking about it for some days. It's possible but not very likely. Quite a few sheep are lost on the moors through natural causes, mostly exposure. Superintendent Holley claims that dogs are responsible for a lot of others, and on top of that there's rustling, which is big business apparently. And to cap it all some sheep disappear into family freezers, I'm told as many as ten sheep a year in some families.'

'That's a hundred sheep per family over ten years. Could be, I suppose, it's a big area. I never knew sheep could disappear on that sort of scale, me being a city boy and all.'

Cole agreed.

'Nor me. What would your Mrs Whatever-her-name-was say to that, I wonder?'

Rogers grinned.

'Something like 'I told you so,' as like as not. Mrs Shore might be knocking on a bit but she's on the ball'. I'd ask her but she moved away some time ago without telling anyone she was going. I heard she didn't go far and she's doing all right, so I imagine she's put herself in a home or something.'

Back at the Incident Room, Mr Cole was informed that Jennifer Wells had been given official permission to take part in the search for Grimalkin and to fly as low as necessary, commensurate with safety. They also discovered that Superintendent Holley had been aloft in her machine while Jenny performed some of the manoeuvres that she had done with Brian Gleaves as a passenger, and the first thing he had done after landing was to demand how much flying lessons would cost him, claiming that he had not enjoyed himself so much for years. He has also seen at first hand some of the problems faced by the aircrews.

PC Croft was present, looking glum as he mentioned how the spring leaves would shortly obscure the view through the trees. When Mr Cole asked him how his sister's bruises were mending he cheered up.

'She's all right sir,' he replied. 'Between you and me she gave as good as she got, she's a blue belt,' he said with a toothy grin.

***

Constable Rogers and Mr Cole reported their progress to Superintendent Holley. After an inspection of the photograph with a powerful magnifying glass he decided that if Grimalkin was in the picture only computer enhancement would show it, so the photograph was marked for laboratory attention.

PC Rogers handed over the typewritten statement of the man who had claimed to have seen Grimalkin at close quarters, with an explanation of his personal opinion of the value of the statement.

Holley agreed.

'I've seen this sort of thing myself, more than once. Someone who claims to be a witness bashes out his own version of events and hands it in on the run. Did he say the facts are all in the statement and he was too busy to answer your stupid questions?'

Peter Cole nodded.

'I thought as much. Did you book him for wasting police time?' Holley asked PC Rogers.

'No sir. I would have on my own patch but not here. He's not the type to plead guilty, he's more likely to make a lot of noise. That doesn't bother me, I've taken some stick before, but I'd have to come all the way from Bath to appear as a witness in a local court and by the time he'd played all the usual tricks like sending in a sick note on the day I'd wind up making half a dozen trips. I thought I'd mark his card and let the local bobby keep an eye on him, but if I'd known at the time that he'd copied this from Mr Cole's book I'd have done him on the spot.'

'Sound thinking. I'll make sure he's seen by one of our own people. Anything else?'

Mr Cole and PC Rogers exchanged glances and both men answered no.

Before he got up to leave Cole mentioned that PC Rogers had been suspicious as soon as he had seen the man, on account of his beard. Superintendent Holley seemed not to be surprised.

'With me it's pipes,' he said, lifting his own pipe out of the out-tray. 'I don't think I've ever arrested a pipe smoker, or seen anyone with hair round his mouth smoke a pipe either. I like that description. 'Hair round his mouth,' it has a sort of feeling about it. How about you Jock?' he asked, swivelling his chair to face Chief Inspector Fillimore.

'Nothing original sir,' Fillimore replied. 'It's what they say, not what they do. When I was in Traffic Division in Yorkshire I used to nick a dozen friends of the chief constable every week. I always made sure it came out in court.'

Addressing Mr Cole he said, 'You stand in the witness box with your book in your hand and you say 'Your Worship, Mr Bloggs then said, 'Officer, I am a personal friend of the chief constable.' It's a veiled threat. Most magistrates take the hint.'

Fillimore laid his pen down and continued, 'As I said, nothing original. I probably share that one with everybody who ever put a uniform on.'

Holley swivelled his chair back to face Peter Cole.

'There you are, that's police prejudice for you. It's a useful tool sometimes.'

Chapter 12

Brian Gleaves parked his pick-up and lifted Button from the seat where she had been curled up asleep until the sound of the handbrake had woken her. He checked the ropes that held three empty oil drums secure in the back of the vehicle, then entered the shop.

A bell rang somewhere and the owner appeared. She stroked the dog, saying, 'Hello Button. Good afternoon Mr Gleaves, what can I do for you today? I saw you on the television with that helicopter and the yellow thing, my goodness it gave me quite a turn, it's a wonder there wasn't an accident. I wouldn't go up in it myself, no I wouldn't. It's not natural, that's what I say.'

Brian was starting to wonder when he was going to get a word in. He held the puppy closer.

'It's for Button,' he said. 'I need some more tins of food and I think some dog biscuits, if she's old enough I mean. I don't know about dogs. Ain't never had a dog before.'

He turned his head as Button licked his face. The woman held out her arms and Brian handed the dog over and replied to questions about her age and background as well as he was able. He didn't know if she had been given any injections but thought it unlikely. He wrote the address of a vet in his grubby notebook as the woman spelled it out.

She looked at the book and said, 'My word, all those figures, you must have been busy.'

'Something I was working out,' Brian answered, not wishing to reveal his aspirations, 'an' here's the drawings what I made for a kennel for Button with a little bit of ground for her to run around on. I don't think she's an indoors dog, not really, she don't seem to like in none in the house all night.'

He showed off his neat drawings.

'I'm sure you're right Mr Gleaves.'

Brian was not used to being called mister and he felt awkward. Still and all, he'd better start getting used to it, things was going to be different from now on, no mistake. He listened to what the woman was saying.

'As long as Button has all the water she needs and she can make her little messes outside the kennel where they can be cleared up, I think she'll do nicely. You will see the vet though, won't you? He can tell you what to do.'

Brian took Button back with thanks and promised to do just that. The woman was still talking as he left the shop.

'Fancy you in that yellow thing. Well I never. It looks dangerous to me. I wouldn't go up in it, not for a pension I wouldn't.'

Brian stopped in the doorway.

'It looks worse than it is really,' he protested.

'Well I don't know, I'm sure,' was the doubtful reply.

Brian escaped thankfully from the shop. She knew her stuff all right but she did go on, he thought.

He was half a mile down the road before he remembered that he had forgotten the tins of food that he had stopped for.

'Can't go without grub mate,' he said, fondling the puppy's ear with his left hand while he looked for a place to turn round. Finding an open farm gate he backed in. Button whimpered and cried a little. Brian was cheerful.

'Come on mate, you'll be all right. She did go on a bit but she wasn't all that bad.'

He enjoyed his little joke. Button covered her nose with her paws and looked trustingly at him. Unblinking green eyes watched them drive away.

***

Brian Gleaves had been telling the truth when he said that Jenny's manoeuvre in the microlight looked worse than it actually was. While Jenny had been flying with Superintendent Holley he had been talking to PC Croft.

'There's limits about what she's allowed to do, an' one thing she ain't allowed to do is dive too steep. Fifty-five degrees is OK, but any steeper is pushing her luck because the Red Arrow ain't built for it. I've been doing some finding out, so I know.'

'I see,' Al Croft lied.

Brian continued, 'Jenny flies at two hundred feet and then she does that dive. I'm goin' to stand out there,' he pointed out of the window, 'and do a bit of figuring, 'cos if I know she starts diving when she crosses the hedge, then I got three angles and one distance, ain't I? So I can say for sure where her wheels will touch the ground, allowin' for a bit of wind an' all. Come on mate, we'll go an' have a look.'

Chief Inspector Fillimore who had watched the proceedings gave his silent assent and said as they left the Incident Room, 'Phew, did anyone know what he was talking about?'

The helicopter crewman, Mike Two, answered him.

'I've seen it done before, or something like it. It usually takes a couple of bods and a theodolite, and a lot of computer hours. Mr Gleaves methods are crude but for an impromtu bash it's not bad. His three angles are ninety degrees vertical, fifty-five degrees for the dive, leaving, uh, thirty-five degrees.'

Mike made a sketch.

'Anyone want to bet he'll be way out in his calculations?'

'Not me,' the chief inspector declined.

'Sergeant?'

Stoke shook his head. There were no takers.

Brian Gleaves did a bit of pacing and said to PC Croft, 'I've got to guess a bit but I reckon as how I ain't far out, an' if I allow a bit o' leeway for her to pull her nose up... Here.'

He stopped pacing and declared, 'In about five minutes mate, she'll touch the ground right level with where I'm standing.'

After the landing he said, 'Don't look so surprised mate, it's all in the figures.'

He carried out his usual thorough inspection and helped Jenny refuel her aircraft and decided that perhaps he had time for a cup of tea in the Mobile Incident Room before attending to his own business.

One of the police officers offered Button a biscuit which she sniffed suspiciously and would not eat before Brian gave it to her himself.

***

It was late evening when he parked outside the hospital and approached the entrance nervously. He stood just inside the door until a bustling nurse stopped long enough to ask him his business, and then summoned a sister. Brian twisted his cap in his hands while he spoke in a voice that the sister had to strain to hear.

'I 'specially came after visiting hours,' he told her. 'I sort of didn't want anyone to see me. It was my boy Ronnie what shot the cat and I sort of had to find out how bad she is. You know.'

He looked at her miserably.

'They say she ain't never coming out,' he added.

Making a swift appraisal the sister took his arm, saying that he could have two minutes, no longer. On the way to the ward she explained the situation and described Rita Windsley's condition sympathetically but plainly. She stood at the foot of the bed where the unseeing girl lay propped on the pillows. Brian looked pale when they left the ward.

'You won't tell them I've come?' he pleaded.

The nursing sister replied, 'Mr Gleaves, it wasn't your fault, you mustn't blame yourself.'

She relaxed her normally severe look.

'What you need is a nice cup of tea. Nurse!' she called, 'A pot of tea in my office. Quickly now!'

Brian left the hospital a little later and on the way home he was overtaken by a pair of speeding police vehicles that he was too upset to notice.

***

It was early morning when the stubble faced superintendent looked out of the window at the confusion of people and vehicles on the road outside farmer Wells' field.

'Looks like the retreat from bloody Moscow,' he grated sourly.

Facing his audience he spoke harshly.

'We're all here so I'll get on with it before I have to let that rabble past the gate.'

He gestured at the scene outside.

'Bloody newspapers,' he added.

There was a shifting of chairs.

'All right then. I'll recap the situation. Last night a dog patrol van got a look at the cat. I've interviewed the driver and this is what happened.'

There was total silence.

Superintendent Holley continued, 'Just off the B3358 the patrol van passed Grimalkin sitting calm as you please by a field gate at the side of the road. The driver stopped and got out and decided to let his dog have a go at it. He was fifty yards up the road and the cat hadn't moved. I don't know what the fool was thinking about but he opened the back of his van, and turned his back on the cat while he did it. That took a few seconds. He opened the door and the next thing he knew was the cat jumped clear over his head and went for the dog. Straight into the back of the van! What took place was short and bloody, you've all seen the inside of the dog van. The dog was torn to pieces, torn to pieces, and when it was over Grimalkin strolled away as casual as you like. A three-legged cat did that. It has a badly injured leg and it took that dog out in a couple of seconds! I'll let Mr Cole do the talking, I think he's got something to say that will make you sit up and take notice. He frightened the daylights out of me.'

There was a stir of interest. Everyone had seen what was in the dog van that was parked outside and some had been present when the dog handler had spent ten very unpleasant minutes in front of the superintendent.

The man was physically uninjured but obviously unfit for duty and some people doubted whether he ever would be. Superintendent Holley had made it clear that he did not want him back, ever.

Peter Cole threaded his way with difficulty through the press of bodies to the front of the room. He looked worried, and there was a hushed silence while everyone waited to hear what he had to say.

'We have entered a new phase,' he began. 'If I may explain,' he surveyed the room, 'Grimalkin has been around for a number of years apparently, and done no harm apart from taking livestock occasionally. The cat avoided contact with human beings and was never seen except by accident. That I call Phase One. Phase Two began the night young Gleaves shot the cat and injured its paw. I'm not happy with his version of what happened but as I think you all know, he's disappeared so he can't be questioned properly. That's a pity, his evidence could be vital. Be that as it may, Phase Two was a defensive posture while Grimalkin licked its wounds, literally, and went to ground. During this phase the cat laid low and the tragic death of the young child was, I believe, a matter of self defence, as was the killing of the farmer's dog.'

Mr Cole let his words sink in. More than one expression hardened at the mention of the death of Steven Windsley, and everyone knew the fate of Rita, whom many had known.

He recalled something that the helicopter captain had told him a day or two previously, putting into words something that he had intuitively grasped already.

'They're letting you have a go with your knock-out gun but don't kid yourself, they look after their own. Their feathers are ruffled and one way or another they're going to get that cat and they don't care what it takes. I don't suppose they've said anything to you, in fact I don't suppose they've said it among themselves, it's one of those things that doesn't need putting into words. It's become personal.'

The captain had added, 'I read that quote in the papers where you said something about an injured cat bent on revenge being the most relentless thing on earth, but you're wrong, Peter. You haven't seen an injured police force in action!'

Peter Cole let his eyes stray over his audience as he recalled those words and marshalled his thoughts. He supposed that revenge had motivated the dog handler who had thought the wounded cat would be an easy kill. He cleared his throat and addressed the room again.

'Phase Three,' he opened, 'is going to be different. Until now the cat has maintained a defensive posture, as I have said already. Last night that changed. I would like to remind you that had Grimalkin chosen to go to cover it could easily have done so. But it didn't, it stayed to slug it out, and it won the first round hands down.'

This was not what his audience wanted to hear. There were angry mutterings that died away under Cole's stare.

'Grimalkin won that round,' he repeated, 'and I don't intend to mince words so I'll tell you straight, your dog man was lucky not to have been killed along with his dog. I'm telling you this in case any of you still think an injured cat is easy game. It isn't. Phase Three is going to be an offensive phase, with Grimalkin taking the initiative. Its behaviour seems more like a jaguar than a leopard, which is what I have believed it to be up until now. I admit that I'm not certain. If it is a jaguar I have more bad news, it could be up to seventy-five pounds heavier than a leopard, and I've said this before but I'll say it again, a jaguar is more inclined to make a fight of it than a leopard is. Keep that in mind!'

Chief Inspector Fillimore took over while Superintendent Holley ran a battery shaver over his face before meeting the press.

'There you have it,' he said bluntly. 'Last night we lost a trained police dog through sheer stupidity and unless we learn fast it might not be a dog next time. If you do see the cat, stay in your vehicles and get on the radio so we can get as many guns as possible to the scene. And keep your eyes open. There's one more thing and this is not, repeat not, to be discussed outside this room. Sometime last night between midnight and six a.m. PC Windsley discharged himself from the hospital via an open window on the ground floor. The only clothing he has is what he went in with, uniform but no headgear. We've put a watch on his home in case he returns there but I have to tell you his mental condition is uncertain, with good reason of course. I repeat, this is not for public consumption.'

He finished briskly.

'Right. You all have your duties. Stay on the radio at all times and keep your eyes and ears open.'

Sergeant Stoke and PC Croft were airborne in the helicopter within minutes.

***

Button barked furiously at a photographer when a flash went off in her face as the constable who was holding back the crowd at the gate let the pick-up through. Jenny Wells waved to Brian as he parked in his usual space and he saw with surprise that she was dressed for flying and the Red Arrow was rolled out. There was no sign of the helicopter. In a few short sentences Jenny told him what had happened.

'I'm flying round the farms in a few minutes,' she informed him. 'Now Grimalkin is on the move they've been on the phone every few minutes so I'll be up and down all day.'

Brian pulled on the flying overall he had taken to wearing whenever he checked her aircraft and remarked that he had better get her started. Jenny laid a hand on his sleeve.

'Brian,' she asked, 'would you mind flying with me? I need company this morning.'

Pausing only long enough to give Button a chocolate drop from the glove box and empty his pockets of loose articles, Brian promised the little dog that he would be back soon and within seconds he was strapping into Jenny's aircraft.

Somewhere over the B3385 they spotted Mr Cole's Range Rover

with the newly painted number on the roof, heading for the scene of the previous night's activity. In the distance the helicopter could be seen flying a search pattern in the area.

***

Superintendent Holley was in a foul mood and seriously contemplating legal action against the manufacturer of the electric razor that had failed to make an impression on his overnight growth of beard stubble. He felt bristly and unwashed, not without cause, and lack of sleep made his eyes red. For once, he looked forward to his retirement.

He snorted to a duty constable, 'I'll speak to that rabble outside, there's no room in here even if I felt like letting them in, which I don't. I'll give them ten minutes and when I tell them to get back on the other side of the hedge I want you and a couple of men to make sure they go. All right, go and let them in.'

He stood on the steps of the helicopter's fuel bowser, where he could see and be seen.

Holley stated the facts briefly and answered what questions he felt able to. Some reporters were hostile, demanding to know when he was going to produce a result. With is temper barely under control he parried the question and concentrated on the fact that Grimalkin was now know for certain to be active and dangerous, and that any hope they might have had that the cat was weakening had disappeared last night.

He allowed pictures to be taken of the locked dog patrol van and wondered for a second or two whether to have it opened as an object lesson. Reluctantly he decided that the chief constable would be less than pleased if he did.

The photographer who had named Grimalkin was present, as always he was with the woman reporter. Together, his information ran, they made a formidable team and it was a toss up whether she would leave her paper to join his or the other way round.

'Are you still reading bed-time stories?' he asked abruptly.

'Not that one,' was the sober reply. 'That story gives me nightmares.'

'Me too.'

Chapter 13

Mr Cole left his vehicle at the side of the road behind a badly parked police vehicle. There was an unmarked vehicle among the police cars and Cole guessed it was a CID car. A police radio on the back seat confirmed his guess. A knot of policemen and women stood at the gate where the police dog handler had spotted Grimalkin the previous night. One or two were smoking; including a CID man wearing plain clothes who seemed to Cole to be making it too obvious that he was armed with a pistol. One of the uniformed men who knew Cole greeted him.

'Morning sir. Come to give us a hand?'

'I've come to see where the police dog was killed,' Cole answered him. 'I thought it might give me some ideas about Grimalkin's next move.'

The CID man butted in with a sneer.

'You don't seem to know much about it,' he said offensively.

Cole looked past him.

'I bet old Gleaves is setting himself up as an expert too, and that bird in the yellow outfit that makes her look like a canary. I've seen you all pretending to know what you're doing.'

He spat at the ground, barely missing Cole's boot, and shrugged the uniformed constable's hand from his arm. Mr Cole turned away and walked back to his Range Rover.

'That's right, we can do without you,' jeered his tormentor.

The uniformed constable caught up with Cole and tried to apologise for his colleague's boorish behaviour.

'Some of those plain clothes boys watch too much television,' he offered by way of explanation. 'They get big ideas.'

Cole compressed his lips and said nothing. He removed his dart firing rifle from his vehicle, stuffed spare ammunition in his pocket, and made his way back to the gate.

He was half way over when the plain clothes man shouted, 'Hey, you! Where do you think you're going?'

Cole sat astride the gate.

'I should have thought that was obvious, even to you,' he replied shortly, feeling irritated with himself for the way he was reacting.

'You can't go over there. That's an order!'

Cole loaded a cartridge into his rifle.

Almost by accident the barrel rested lightly on the plain-clothes man's shoulder for as long as it took Cole to say through gritted teeth, 'Mind whom you try to give orders to Sonny, and put your toy away before somebody gets hurt.'

He slipped to the ground and walked away, following the line of the hedge as he searched for anything that would give him a clue where the cat was. Hearing an angry shout behind him he ignored it and walked on.

Some time later the helicopter passed close by him, and he ignored that as well. It was too early to be sure, but at last he thought he knew what the cat was going to do next.

Sergeant Stoke saw him from the helicopter, walking along a hedgerow. In the distance Jenny's wing flashed as she banked steeply over one of the farms she watched over.

***

The kitchen clock struck a quarter to the hour, causing George Wells to look at his own watch with surprise.

'Later than I thought,' he observed. 'It always takes me a while to get my books done. I'll do the rounds in a minute.'

'Harry said he'd go with you,' Mrs Wells replied as she filled the kettle.

Harry Stoke and Jenny were watching television in the living room. Jenny had been flying on and off until nightfall when all flying ceased for the day and she looked tired. After her first trip with Brian Gleaves for company she had flown solo. On the ground and in the air it had been a frustrating day.

David Windsley was still missing. He had not returned home and enquiries with his and Rita's families and friends had drawn a blank. The police reluctantly informed the media and the evening news had made a big thing of it. It was no secret that things were not going well.

A short clip of film showed the microlight passing overhead. It must have been taken during Jenny's flight with Brian Gleaves because two heads were clearly visible.

George Wells put his head round the door.

'The kettle should have boiled by the time we get back if we start the rounds now,' he said, and added 'I'll take my gun. I can unlock yours too if you like.'

Stoke stood up.

'I've got the Viking gun in the boot of my car, I'll use that, it's a bit handier, especially with grapeshot in both barrels.'

Wells agreed and acknowledged that he felt happier with Harry Stoke guarding his back.

They walked in single file, Wells covering the front and left, and Stoke guarding the right and rear. Under other circumstances they would have felt ridiculous at 'playing soldiers' but nobody was taking chances now Grimalkin had gone on the offensive. The safety catches were off both weapons.

Apart from a restless ewe the paddock was quiet and none of the flock appeared nervous. They patrolled all the buildings, including Jenny's hangar. George Wells shone his torch across the front of the building. Everything was secure and nothing disturbed the silence of the night.

Keeping warily alert they began the walk back to the farmhouse. Neither gun would be unloaded until they stood outside the back door. There was a sudden movement behind them.

Stoke flung himself to one side and rolled, coming up with the Viking gun pulled hard into his shoulder and his finger on the trigger. He slotted the luminous foresight into the U-shaped notch of the rearsight. With a flurry of beating wings a night bird took flight with a raucous squawk. Stoke was not surprised to see George Wells on one knee with his gun aimed at the spot where he had been standing. Each man let his breath out slowly. There was nothing to be said.

Stoke stayed at the house long enough to drink a last cup of unsweetened coffee, then left.

Tomorrow would be another long day.

***

Brian Gleaves wiped his hands on a waste rag, his dirt-smeared arms glistening with sweat in the light beneath the naked bulb. It was a relief to stop the laborious pumping of the waste fuel and oil from the sump beneath the floor of his workshop. One of the oil drums that he had brought in was full and he frowned doubtfully at the washer under the screw-threaded cap.

He said to Button, 'That there's a fibre washer and it ain't a lot of use but it came with the drum an' it's all I've got so it'll have too do, won't it? Expect it'll take up some spillage and expand and then it'll be all right. Leastaways like, I hope it will. I done my best, anyway.'

Button wagged her tail.

'What's that mate? Cut a new washer? Well I 'spect I could, only I ain't got the right stuff. Can't use rubber and I'll tell you why. Rubber rots in petrol, that's why. It'd hold for a while but it ain't professional like. Won't do.'

Putting the rag down he said, 'Come on mate, time to jack it in I reckon. You got any water in your bowl? Let's 'ave a look, shall we?'

Brian locked the workshop and put Button to bed in her kennel for the night, closing the gate on the dog pound with care before heading for the house.

'Could do with a beer after all that,' he told himself.

***

Far away, an ex-detective constable who had suddenly found himself back in uniform after he had deliberately aimed a loaded pistol at Peter Cole's back earlier in the day cursed his luck and wondered what he was going to say to the disciplinary board.

***

The paw was healing well. The cat would always walk with a bad limp but the suppuration had ceased and the healing process continued. The agonising throb had gone and provided there was no further infection the cat was going to be all right. Grimalkin had rabbit for dinner.

Chapter 14

Brian Gleaves looked upset as the policeman at the gate waved him through and he drove into the field in the early afternoon. He sat in his pick-up until PC Croft came to see what was keeping him.

'Sorry mate. Had a rough morning,' was the muttered reply.

'Button's all right, isn't she?' Croft asked earnestly.

The dog was becoming a pet of the police who staffed the Incident Room.

'It ain't her. I might as well tell you I 'spose. I went to them courts this morning. Ronnie was meant to be there, you know? Anyway I went along to tell them I ain't seen him.'

'You needn't have, you could have phoned. You didn't even have to do that if you didn't want to.'

'Well I thought I better. Them magistrates weren't very nice about it. Worst of all was them reporters and stuff what was waiting for Ronnie to turn up. They all crowded round me when I came out an' I couldn't even get back to me van.'

Brian sounded miserable.

'And there was all them cameras and flash bulbs and things and I ain't never done nothing and one of your lot stopped me getting away and gave me a ticket or something and now I've got to take my licence and stuff to the police station.'

He fumbled in his top pocket and found a creased slip of paper, which he unfolded and read, pointing at the words with his stubby finger.

'Me driving licence and MOT certificate and insurance and all and I tried to show them to him and he just gave me this ticket.'

He sounded aggrieved and bewildered.

'Did you have them with you?'

PC Croft's tone was sharper than he intended.

Brian Gleaves took his papers out of the glove box and it took Croft only seconds to confirm that everything about the documents was in order.

'I 'spose I still have to take them in?' Brian asked dully.

''Fraid so mate.'

But PC Croft made a note of the name and number of the issuing officer, and as far as he was concerned the ex-detective constable who was going out of his way to make trouble had just made some. To his own astonishment PC Croft had developed a lot of respect for Brian Gleaves and he was beginning to think that maybe he deserved a better deal. He was aware that the little man was painfully shy among strangers and attending the Magistrates Court must have been an ordeal. There was no need for anyone to mess him about. Croft would have a word with Sergeant Stoke.

He suggested the kettle might be on in the Incident Room if they got a move on, adding, 'I'm not having any though, I'm up in the helicopter later and I made that mistake yesterday. I got through the last half hour with my legs crossed but it was touch and go!'

Button sniffed an interesting lump of mud before bounding up the steps of the Incident Room. Al Croft remarked that if the mobile trailer was not moved soon it would sink into the mud that was churned up by the constant passage of feet.

'Had to push old Dan Horrocks when he brought the milk this morning,' he said, 'but that milk float is clapped out anyway.'

A map was spread across the table and when they opened the door the helicopter captain said to Brian, 'That's your place isn't it? We'll be flying close by this afternoon.'

Brian took a few moments to get orientated with the map.

'Next time you come up with us we can fly right over if you like,' the pilot promised.

Brian looked pleased. He had not expected to be invited into the helicopter again.

'I wouldn't mind that,' he said eagerly.

'Well remember what I taught you the other day because it's your turn to do the flying,' the pilot joked. 'I'll be in the back, playing cards with Mike!'

When he straightened up from the table a photograph fell to the floor. Button nosed at it and uttered a series of sharp barks and fled with her tail between her legs, and cowered in a corner where she whimpered and pressed herself hard against the wall.

PC Croft picked her up.

Chief Inspector Fillimore examined the photograph with a strange expression on his face. According to the note on his desk it was an enlargement of the photograph that the colour-blind woman had given to PC Rogers and Mr Cole. The note added that computer enhancement had been inconclusive.

Returning it to a folder Fillimore remarked that perhaps there was something in it after all.

'Perhaps we should try it on that Sheba brute when the dog handler gets here,' he said.

Brian Gleaves smiled inwardly at the mention of the police dog's name. He remained on the site until the helicopter took off and then left to continue pumping out the sump under his workshop, which looked like being a bigger job than he had thought. The bottom was ankle deep in sludge. It was late when he finished work for the day. He shut Button in her kennel and removed the axe from his chopping block so he could sit on it for a few minutes and talk to her while she settled for the night. Only then did he get up and go indoors, laying the axe down gently so as not to disturb the sleeping dog.

***

During the night the weather changed as a weak front swept slowly over the moors. There was no wind to speak of and low cloud drifted penetrating drizzle everywhere. A telephone conversation with the Incident Room confirmed that the microlight was grounded until the weather improved, probably by mid or late afternoon, and the helicopter was on stand-by only and would not fly unless the cat was seen, which seemed unlikely as visibility on the moors was measured in inches.

Brian Gleaves had work to do, work which he had been putting off while he attended to other things, like pumping waste oil and servicing the microlight. There was not much machinery in the workshop but a few jobs were waiting and Brian decided not to do any more pumping for the time being. It was a backbreaking and monotonous task.

Some of the machinery would be needed now that spring had come so he spent the morning with a grease gun in his hand. When the post arrived it included a thick brown envelope that Brian ripped open and read avidly.

The grey drizzle soaked into everything it touched. Button stood in the doorway and decided that she was better off where she was, so she took her chewing strip and curled up on a piece of sacking material.

***

The light in the Incident Room was bad and Mr Cole sat by a window while he made notes, often referring to an ordnance survey map and measuring distances. The theory he had begun to develop was taking shape and he felt excited. At last he was making progress, though it was a little premature to announce his findings. He needed more time. All the same, he thought he was getting somewhere. He felt guilty about concealing his ideas, however tentative, but he did not want to start a wild goose chase so he kept quiet.

He could see Harry Stoke pacing up and down outside, oblivious to the weather that drifted like heavy curtains across the fields and made the bright windsock cling wetly to its mast.

Stoke found the inaction frustrating and it was no secret that he felt that he had not made much of a contribution to the hunt for Grimalkin so far, though he had spent all his waking hours on the job.

His flying time in both aircraft was mounting up to an impressive number of hours. Both his guns, the Viking shotgun and the Parker-Hale with the telescopic sight, were in the Incident Room where they could be snatched up at a moment's notice.

Peter Cole knew that his own chances of knocking out Grimalkin and capturing the big cat were vanishingly small.

The radio link was temporarily manned by PC Croft while the senior police officers did some halfhearted paperwork, and occasionally the superintendent missed the waste bin with his spent matches,

The day wore on. By mid-afternoon the sky lightened and the weather turned dryer. The helicopter flew a sortie that confirmed what everybody knew already, that cloud covered the high ground and made operations impossible. Harry Stoke stared at the ground as they flew just beneath the cloudbase with grey wisps flashing by the open door as they patrolled the farms that Jenny in her microlight was not able to get to in these conditions. There was nothing to see and the aircraft was back on the ground within forty-five minutes of take off. There would be no more flying that day. Stoke and Croft assisted the crew to fit covers over the cockpit windows and the engine inlets and exhausts.

The policemen came into the Incident Room, which the flying crew still insisted on calling the caravan, and wiped their various weapons dry with lightly oiled cloths. Stoke locked the Viking gun in the boot of his car and made sure that he had a spare set of batteries for his personal radio.

He spent a couple of hours fruitlessly pacing up and down and went off duty as the light failed.

An improvement in flying conditions was promised. Stoke hoped the forecast was reliable.

Hours later when Superintendent Holley was about to go off duty the phone rang with the news that David Windsley had turned up at his home and slipped in past the police constable who had spotted the light go on behind drawn curtains. He failed to answer when the constable rang the bell.

***

Lingering cloud drifted off the high ground and swept northwards towards the Bristol Channel. Watery sunshine followed. Most police officers still wore rain gear. Dan Horrocks, when he delivered the milk, did not risk becoming bogged again in the churned mud that was the only entrance to the field where the hunt for Grimalkin had its headquarters.

As he stodged his way out with a wire basket filled with empty bottles he received a splash of muddy water from a passing police vehicle and was still muttering under his breath when Brian Gleaves stopped alongside his milk float and asked how much he owed, saying truthfully, 'I ain't been around when the milk was brought so I couldn't square it up, could I?' as he counted his coins.

Dan Horrocks took the money and entered the amount in his account book.

'Mr Windsley, he's come back,' he volunteered.

Brian Gleaves turned to look at the Incident Room and old Dan added, 'Not here I don't mean, but I just heard them lot in there say he's turned up at home and I dunno if I'm supposed to deliver there or not. Funny do if you ask me,' he concluded.

Sergeant Stoke confirmed what Dan Horrocks had said.

'He returned home last night and he hasn't left as far as I know. Where he's been is anyone's guess. He told the force welfare officer he's OK and shut the door in his face and they've put a copper outside his gate in a plain car and told him to talk to him if he changes his mind. At the moment that's about all they can do.'

Stoke was clearly unhappy about it.

When Button had been petted by everybody and surreptitiously fed a square of chocolate by the superintendent as she nosed the spent matches around his waste bin, Brian made his way to Jenny's hangar on foot, finding the door open. He helped her bring her aircraft out and talked about the mail he had received the previous day while he inspected it.

'I've got all that stuff about licences what I asked for and a lot more besides,' he said, looking pleased.

Brian wondered whether the wet ground would hamper Jenny's take off. She thought not.

'I'm not heavy enough to sink in. I might need a few extra feet to get airborne, but it's no trouble,' she said confidently.

The helicopter was airborne first, heading for the moors with Stoke and Croft on board. Peter Cole stood and watched until it was out of sight.

Button dropped her chewing strip at Jenny's feet and Jenny played with the puppy while Brian continued to inspect the aircraft. Brian talked while he worked.

'I'll be going over to Bristol today to my sister's place but I don't expect I'll stay as long as usual. Probably come back as soon as I've had a bite of breakfast. Got to get back to Button because I'm leaving her in her kennel because she ain't a dog what likes being indoors and it ain't fair to make her stay where she don't like it.'

He was not expecting a reply, just making talk.

'I'll be showing my sister all that stuff what I got sent and I don't expect she'll hardly believe it when she hears about me flying and everything. Can't hardly believe it myself.'

He sounded pleased and proud.

Jenny tugged the chewing strip as Button held the other end firmly between her teeth and pulled hard in the other direction with her tail wagging furiously.

She said without looking up, 'I'm going to fly this morning to look at the farms and this afternoon I'm taking Harry up. Father had a phone call from Mr Cole and he says he thinks Grimalkin is on the move again. Brian, I'll be glad when this is over and we can get back to normal.'

Too late, she realised that for a lot of people, including Brian Gleaves, things would never be the same again but he did not seem to take her words badly. He agreed with her. Wiping the wheels clean of all traces of mud he stuffed his cleaning rag deep into one of the leg pockets of his flying overall. They made their way to the Incident Room.

Peter Cole was inside, repeating to Superintendent Holley what he had said to George Wells on the telephone, that he thought the cat was on the move again, adding that he hoped to be able to prove it later in the day.

Jenny gave her flight plan to Chief Inspector Fillimore at his radio link. In return he provided her with the locations and roof numbers of all the vehicles in her area and informed them and the helicopter that the microlight would shortly be operating.

Soon after watching Jenny take off Brian left for home, to see to Button and change his clothes before he set off to Bristol. Catching sight of his vehicle, Jenny watched it for a few moments before continuing her patrol.

She landed an hour later after an uneventful flight.

Chapter 15

Suppressing his feelings of guilt Peter Cole locked his Range Rover and slipped the keys into his jacket pocket. He had left details of where he was going with Chief Inspector Fillimore at his radio link and he carried a police issue personal radio but it was not always possible to get through on the air because the rolling moors created dead spots where the radio was useless. These dead spots could extend for miles, and as he discovered when he tried to contact the Incident Room, he was in one now.

He had said where he was going, but not why, and that was the reason he felt guilty now. At last he thought he stood a good chance of finding Grimalkin, and knowing how the police felt about the cat he wanted to reach the animal first.

The prospect was exciting and terrifying.

Mr Cole had no illusions about the cat but his eagerness to solve one puzzle drove him on. The puzzle was Grimalkin's identity. Try as he might, Peter Cole had no real idea what sort of cat he was hunting. He did know one thing; Grimalkin really was a witch's cat.

He loaded a cartridge into his gun, wishing that it held more than just one round at a time, but it was not really meant for this kind of work. He was about to set off onto the moors when a van drove past and he stood behind his Range Rover until it was gone. There was no need to draw attention to himself.

The legend on the side of the van informed him that it belonged to a window cleaner, and a ladder poked out from inside the vehicle. The driver stared at the Range Rover as he passed.

One last check with the map and compass and Cole was on his way, keeping alert as he walked slowly uphill. There was no hurry, nothing would be gained by rushing and he had a lot of ground to cover. Best take things easy. He tried the radio again, panting as the trail was steeper than it appeared, but there was no response.

Peter Cole was not surprised. He was a long way from base and even if the terrain had been level he was at the limits of radio range. Perhaps he would be able to make contact later.

He estimated that he could keep the cat unconscious for no longer than twenty minutes. Long enough to summon assistance, if only he could use his radio. If he could not, well that was something he did not want to think about.

Cole took his finger off the transmit button and walked on, panting with exertion and trying to pace himself.

It looked like being a long afternoon.

***

Brian Gleaves made his preparations for his monthly trip to Bristol to visit his sister. There was a little money to take, not much this month because Ronnie had taken it with him when he disappeared and Brian had not had much coming in recently. What with everything else he had not got a lot of work done, but he wanted to do his bit in the hunt for Grimalkin so he had not taken much on. Besides, there was all that waste oil to be pumped out and got rid of first. The laboriously filled oil drums were still in the workshop, waiting to be taken away. As he had expected, there was some seepage from the filler caps, which he wiped off and left the rag on top of a drum for further use.

The cover was still off the sump, there was no point in putting it back, he would have to shift the pump and re-prime it before he could start to pump again. Better to leave it. He shut the workshop door and locked it.

There was a lot to be taken to Bristol. All the stuff that had come in the post for one thing, he wanted his sister to see it. And his flying overall, mustn't forget that!

He made sure Button was secure in her pound. There was plenty of water and she had just been fed so she would not be hungry before he came back. She gnawed her chewing strip and ignored the rubber bone that Brian had purchased at the same time. She had never liked the bone much.

Brian stood with one foot on his chopping block, resting his elbow on his knee.

'Get a good night's sleep,' he said, 'we got work to do tomorrow. I reckon one good day an' we can shift them drums and get the pumping finished.'

The puppy regarded him with solemn eyes and wagged her tail.

***

A few miles down the road Brian Gleaves detoured from his route and called at a florist where he spent some time making a careful selection.

He arrived at his sister's home later than usual, letting himself in because his sister was still out doing her Saturday shopping. Over the years he had established a routine and he filled the kettle, ready to boil the water a few minutes before his sister got off the bus at the end of the road, and set out cups and saucers.

On his last visit he had replaced a cracked window in the bathroom, and he tested the putty with his thumbnail. It would take a coat of paint whenever he was ready to do it and he pencilled a note in his book to remind himself to bring paint with him next time he came. Should really have thought of it before but what with everything else it had just sort of slipped his mind.

He sat down with the envelope that contained all the material he had been sent about microlight and other aircraft. There was a lot of stuff and he wanted to read it over again. When he heard his sister unlock the door he jumped to his feet with the realisation that he had not boiled the water yet. Hastily he flipped the switch and went to help with the shopping bags, and found that he had to find answers to a barrage of questions about what he had been up to. Well, first he'd better get the tea poured, because it was a long story.

Later, in the cosy front room with the curtains drawn against the night chill, his sister sat and poked the red coals on the fire. Leaflets and technical brochures were scattered on the floor. There were lots of pictures of microlight aircraft.

Brian was finishing his story.

'So that's what happened Marge,' he said. 'Blimey, I never thought I'd be flying around and all. And those pictures on the telly!'

'Made me feel faint,' his sister declared.

Brian told her all about Button and how he came to change her name from Sheba, and then Marge wanted to hear all about the people he had been with. She had met Superintendent Holley several times when she had stayed at Brian's house when he had a nasty touch of flu, which kept him in bed for a week. He had been an inspector then. She heard about Jenny Wells and her aircraft, and the trip to the flying club, and finally Brian told her about Sergeant Harry Stoke.

'I can't exactly figure him out,' he confessed. 'He's Jenny's boyfriend and I expect they'll get married before long. It's the other things I can't get straight in my mind. He's a tough one but he don't try it on if you get my meaning. He don't give the orders neither but he wouldn't let anyone else fly in Jenny's Red Arrow after I sort of thought the cat might be used to seeing it. I reckon he's your man if you want something done in a hurry, and I don't think what crowns and things you had on your shoulders would count for much. He's sort of easy going most of the time but I wouldn't want to get on the wrong side of him. One thing, he's straight, dead straight. Do right by Sergeant Stoke and he'll do right by you.'

Marge poked the fire some more and settled comfortably in her armchair.

Brian had reached a decision.

'I'm going to clear my slate when this is done. I sort of want to start fresh,' he said.

'I always said you should have done it a long time ago,' was his sister's reply.

Brian Gleaves stared into the flames.

'Way things have turned out, maybe I should,' he said slowly.

***

Jenny was dressed for flying as she usually was, but Harry Stoke wore a disruptive pattern jacket. As he had said before, Jenny wanted to be highly visible but he did not. He wanted Grimalkin to be driven towards him so that he could get a clear shot at the cat at close range, and wearing bright clothes like Jenny's would put an end to any chance of that. Besides, this jacket had deep pockets where he could keep a supply of cartridges for the double-barrelled Viking shotgun that he carried when he flew with Jenny.

Permission had been obtained for him to fly with the gun provided it was not loaded but Sergeant Stoke was in the habit of loading special grapeshot into both barrels as soon as they were clear of the ground. Jenny pursed her lips but said nothing.

They studied the map before they got airborne and Chief Inspector Fillimore showed them where Peter Cole was thought to be. It was not in the area where Grimalkin had been seen before and they were curious to know what Cole was up to. He had hinted that he knew what the cat was doing but had declared that he did not know where it was. Jenny thought she would be able to find his Range Rover. She had seen it in the morning and knew it was headed in the general direction of where Cole had said he would be, so provided he was still there she would be able to find him.

Fillimore had not been able to raise him on the radio, but he was aware of the difficulties. Stoke put his own radio in his pocket, with the comment that he might be able to get through with the advantage of height.

Before getting into the aircraft Jenny inspected the soles of her boots and Harry Stoke do the same. Both had collected heavy mud on their soles and Jenny would not have it in her machine. Stoke said a few words into his radio and a policewoman came running with a wooden ruler. They scraped their boots clean.

Jenny's take off was as smooth as usual but the air was unexpectedly cold.

Jenny felt it too and her voice in Stoke's helmet said calmly, 'We're feeling the effects of a cold front.'

Stoke was too busy to reply, he was loading cartridges into his gun. They flew low. The first stage of the flight included a tour of the farms and they sighted several men with shotguns in some fields. Jenny circled a small group who all waved.

Stoke said, 'Have you noticed how they all stick together?'

Jenny had not thought much about it but agreed that it was true. Mr North's cattle had a full trough of water, which reminded Stoke of something.

'You don't feel like starting a stampede?' he asked.

Jenny sounded surprised as she turned to look at him, round eyed behind her goggles.

'Who told you?'

'You're not the only one who does the rounds. One of our boys heard it from Mrs North when he called there. You told Mr North his trough was dry again and if he let it happen once more you'd stampede his cattle all over the moors.'

Stoke sounded amused.

'He knows I wouldn't. But it was the third or fourth time and his cows needed a drink.'

Jenny needed all her concentration at low level and Stoke had thoughts of his own. There was little talk.

When all the farms had been checked Jenny dipped her wing to a farmer's wife who waved from her doorstep, and raised the nose of the microlight slightly as she made a wide sweeping turn that brought the moors into full view. As they gained height Harry Stoke felt one of Jenny's hands reaching for his and he gave her fingers an affectionate squeeze.

'We haven't had much time in the last few days.'

'I know. We've both been busy.'

'I'm missing you.'

'Me too.'

Stoke recognised the bend in the road that was one of Jenny's navigation points, though on this occasion she did not make the usual turn for home.

'I'm going for more height. We ought to be somewhere near Mr Cole in about ten minutes, maybe fifteen. It should be easier to see his Range Rover with a couple more thousand feet underneath us.'

Harry Stoke agreed.

A blue roofed van made slow progress up a steep hill below. He watched it struggle up the slope.

Chapter 16

Peter Cole's Range Rover took some time to find. Harry Stoke eventually spotted it on a narrow road at the junction with a moorland trail, parked against a steep bank that was topped by a hedge. Jenny circled, losing height until she was almost brushing the treetops. There was no sign of Peter Cole. Jenny opened the throttle and climbed.

'I'll take us to five hundred feet and circle round.'

'How are we for fuel?'

'About an hour, plus a safety margin. He can't be that far away.'

Jenny flew in widening circles, scanning the ground anxiously. The moors were deserted. Jenny tapped her wristwatch.

'I'm getting worried Harry. We should have seen something by now.'

'I know. Jenny love, I think we're looking in the wrong place. Go back to the Range Rover and head straight along that trail. He might have gone further than we think.'

Jenny abandoned her search pattern and put the Red Arrow into a tight turn. They picked up the Range Rover and the start of the trail.

Neither she nor Stoke had seen anything when she spoke after five minutes.

'We've been out this far before, when I was going round in circles. What shall I do now?'

'Keep going. We're miles from anywhere. I'm running out of ideas,' Stoke admitted. He added, 'We might see more if we go higher.'

'OK. I'm down to forty-five minutes plus reserves Harry, and it's a long way home. We can't stay out here much longer.'

'Uh huh. We're going in the right direction, more or less. Keep going until we reach the main road and then we'll go home. Can you do that?'

'Just.'

Stoke was concerned. They ought to have seen something and he wondered if Cole had managed to get lost. It was not difficult on the moors. There was nothing below the aircraft except miles of springy heather.

Jenny saw him first. Harry Stoke was so intent on searching the ground directly below that he failed to hear Jenny until she tapped his knee.

'Over there on the edge of that clear patch by the bridleway. I'll lose some height.'

'How the hell did he get right out here?'

'He's seen us, he's waving.'

'Well at least he's all right. I was getting worried.'

Jenny began a long descent with the engine throttled right back while the lonely figure on the moors continued to wave both arms. Jenny circled overhead, then gasped.

'Harry, it's the cat! Look!'

Stoke spotted Grimalkin at the same instant. Cole was being stalked.

'Bloody hell, he can't see it! We've got to scare it off!'

Jenny slammed the throttle wide open and dived in an attempt to fly right over the cat and drive it off. Peter Cole stood and watched.

'He thinks we're playing silly buggers!'

Stoke slipped the catch off the Viking gun and fired both barrels.

'Did you hit it?' Jenny shouted.

'No, I was trying to scare it away and let Peter know. Look, he's caught on!' Stoke shouted back at her.

Peter Cole took a few stumbling paces. The microlight was nearly overhead when he changed direction and made for the centre of the small clearing with the obvious intent of giving himself a chance of spotting Grimalkin as the cat approached.

He turned and walked warily backwards with his gun held ready. The horror stricken occupants of the microlight could only watch and shout.

'Behind you! It's behind you!'

Grimalkin sprang.

Peter Cole was hit from behind and thrown to the ground, the cat on top of him with its fangs sunk into his shoulder and both rear legs clawing like pistons, tearing his flesh to ribbons.

'Get me down fast!' Stoke yelled. 'Get me down there!'

Jenny clenched her teeth and yanked the Red Arrow into a vicious turn with one wingtip brushing the heather. She aimed straight at the cat that was mauling the still figure of Peter Cole as he lay face down on the grass.

Barely feet away, she cut the power to the engine and heaved her nose skywards, using the whole of her wing as a brake. It was asking for trouble and Jenny knew the risk she was taking. Forcing the nose back down she slammed her wheels into the turf and put every ounce of her strength into applying the brakes.

She had heard bad landings described as controlled crashes and she knew she had got away with it through sheer good luck. She had over-stressed every part of the Red Arrow but this was not the time to worry about that. A detached part of her mind told her that she would have to get Brian Gleaves to overhaul it thoroughly before she flew again. And she would pay him properly.

Stoke was out of the machine and running. The cat had gone and she had not even noticed.

Harry Stoke crouched beside the stricken man and scanned the area alertly before laying his gun down. Cole was unconscious and bleeding from a dozen deep gashes in his upper leg, soaking his ripped trousers in blood that was seeping into the grass.

'You look at his shoulder, I'll try and stop the bleeding!' Stoke rapped at Jenny who did as she was told and replied unsteadily, 'He's not hurt badly around his shoulder Harry, his jacket saved him, but his breathing isn't good and,' she dropped the limp hand she was holding, 'his pulse is weak. Harry, he's going to die!'

'No he isn't!' Stoke snapped. 'Can you fly him out of here?'

Jenny bit her lip.

'I think so. Yes.'

Stoke stripped off his jacket.

'Good. Press just here where I was holding him. I'm going to try and stop the bleeding.'

He laid his coat out and rolled it up tightly from the bottom hem and pressed it firmly against Cole's horrific wounds, using the sleeves to bind it tightly.

'How's he doing?'

'Still breathing.'

'Good girl. Help me get him strapped in.'

The struggling pair carried the unconscious man to the microlight with drops of blood staining the ground all the way. It was going to be touch and go, Peter Cole would be lucky to survive the massive blood loss.

Stoke noticed that Cole had a radio slung around his neck. He quickly exchanged it for his own, which he knew was serviceable. Cole's might not be. As Jenny strapped herself into the aircraft he thrust it into the pocket of her yellow suit just above her left knee. The short stubby aerial poked out.

'Use that. Let them know you're coming. Just press the button and talk. Got that?' he yelled above the roar of the engine as Jenny got her propeller spinning.

Without waiting for a reply he dashed out of the way as Jenny ran the engine up to full throttle and released the brakes.

The ground was rough and the clearing was small. Stoke held his breath as the microlight staggered into the air far too slowly. A wing dipped, the aircraft wobbled and Stoke could hardly bear to watch as Jenny lost most of the precious few feet between the microlight and the ground. Somehow she kept herself in the air and made a risky flat turn that allowed her to fly downhill until she gained enough speed to pull up the nose and steer in the right direction.

Weakly, Stoke exhaled his pent up breath.

He tested Cole's radio, which seemed to be working although he got no response to his transmission. Running to pick up his dropped gun he remembered with a hollow feeling that he had discharged both barrels from the air and not reloaded, and his spare ammunition had just gone with his jacket.

The hairs on the back of his neck rose as he muttered, 'Bloody hell!'

There was still Cole's weapon, which was better than nothing. It did not take Stoke long to find it. He opened the breech and ejected a spent cartridge.

***

Jenny found it hard to control her aircraft as she left Harry Stoke behind in the clearing and lifted into the air. The controls were mushy and she dared not look at the instruments to check her airspeed. There was no need, it was too low and she knew it.

The ground fell away below her as she followed the downhill slope and gradually reached a safe flying speed. Setting a new course she kept the throttle wide open and stayed low. There was no time to waste in gaining height and in any event she had the height of the moors to lose before she reached her airfield.

Risking a swift look at Peter Cole she could see he was deathly pale and still, and she leaned forward in her seat in a desperate and futile attempt to go faster, the engine screaming protest at the rough handling she gave it. She checked her course. It was easy to stray at low level and she reluctantly decided to add a couple of hundred feet to her height, sacrificing a little speed to do so. That was better, and now she could fly an exact course to her airfield.

The aerial sticking out of her pocked reminded her that she had Harry Stoke's radio and she fumbled it out of her pocket. She did not listen for a reply; she could not hear anything with her helmet covering her ears and the noise of the engine bellowing at full throttle behind her. She pushed own the transmit button and yelled into the radio.

'This is Jenny Wells in the Red Arrow. Mr Cole is badly hurt and I'm bringing him in!'

Still holding the radio she looked once again at Peter Cole, seeing with horror that he was sitting in a pool of blood that was whipped about by the rushing wind. She realised that there was nothing she could do to prevent him from bleeding to death while she watched helplessly.

'This is Jenny Wells. He's bleeding!'

Jenny knew that her message was pointless and hysterical.

Superintendent Holley reacted swiftly to the garbled messages that came out of the receiver.

'Have a car ready. And try to find out what's happened to Stoke!'

Jenny was frantic.

'I can't stop the bleeding!'

Her voice rose shrilly and Chief Inspector Fillimore tried without success to speak to her.

'This is Jenny Wells in the Red Arrow. I can't stop the bleeding and he's going to die!'

Like a hunted animal she searched for some way to escape from the situation she found herself in. She stared intently at the ground and in a flash her mind was made up.

'This is Jenny in the Red Arrow. I'm going to land on the B3224. This is Jenny in the Red Arrow. I'm going to land on the B3224!'

There was no time to wonder if her message had been received.

Her aircraft bounced and slewed across the road as she slammed it down in front of a badly shaken driver who stamped on his brake pedal and swerved onto the verge to avoid a collision, sliding sideways and skidding to a stop with a squeal of tortured tyres.

Jenny unstrapped and was trying to staunch Peter Cole's bleeding when the driver raced up to the microlight.

'What the hell do you think... Christ Almighty!'

There was blood all over the place.

The driver grasped the situation in seconds, shouting, 'Help me get him into my car!'

Jenny desperately retied the sleeves of Harry Stoke's jacket around Cole's upper leg, trying to put on enough pressure to stop the life draining flow of blood. They managed to lift him out of the microlight and stagger to the car with the dead weight of the unconscious body.

Red faced with exertion the driver gasped, 'Open the door!'

As Jenny obeyed his order she saw with a shock of surprise that there was a front seat passenger who had not made a move to help and her eyes blazed with anger. The driver leaned into the car, pushing Cole into the back seat while Jenny rushed to the other side and flung the door open so she could pull from her side. The passenger began to protest.

'This is a company car. All that mess, you can't...'

'Shut up!' the driver snapped. 'And help me shift that aeroplane out of the way.'

To Jenny he ordered, 'Stay here and take care of him.'

Pulling a sample case off the floor to give Jenny a little more room he hurled it away, and it burst open at the side of the road. Ignoring the bleating protests of his passenger he shoved the man towards Jenny's Red Arrow and set to clearing the road.

A two-tone siren seemed to Jenny to be sounding off in her ear and the next second a policeman leaned across Peter Cole. The car driver raced up behind him.

'We've got to get him to hospital,' he said urgently.

'I'll drive, you get in the other side.'

To the erstwhile passenger the policeman ordered, 'Stay here and keep an eye on that plane.'

He leaped into the driving seat and waved on the patrol car that had brought him.

'Clear the road,' he yelled. 'Minehead hospital!'

The acceleration threw Jenny against her seat.

In near normal tones the police officer said, 'We heard you on the radio and we weren't far away. How's he doing?'

'I don't know.'

Jenny's voice shook.

The former driver, now sitting in the passenger seat, turned round and managed to kneel on the seat and bend over Peter Cole, saying over his shoulder, 'He's still bleeding. I'll put some pressure on.'

His strong hands gripped Cole's thigh.

'That might do it.'

A police motorcycle howled past, siren blaring, making Jenny jump. She wondered how the policeman driving the car could sound so calm as he drove flat out.

'There goes the cavalry. My name's Jones by the way. You must be Jenny Wells.'

'Yes,' Jenny replied without looking up.

She was still doing as much as she could for Peter Cole.

'I'm Reg Collins,' the civilian holding Cole's leg said, 'and I'll be obliged if you don't brake suddenly or I'll go arse first through the windscreen. Pardon me,' he added to Jenny.

'I think I've stopped the bleeding,' he continued, 'see if you can get at his wallet, it might save time if we know his blood group.'

Numbly Jenny did as she was told. There was nothing in Cole's wallet to indicate his blood group.

'Pity, but we couldn't get on the radio and tell anyone anyway.'

'Yes we could!' Jenny exclaimed. 'I've got Harry's radio. Sergeant Stoke,' she added hastily.

Without slackening speed the driver flung the car into a corner, still talking as calmly as if he were sitting at home in his armchair, but managing to sound urgent at the same time.

'Use it quick. Tell the boss where Sergeant Stoke is!'

With a shock that hit like a shower of cold water Jenny realised that Harry Stoke was left on the moors with Grimalkin - and she had his radio.

Somehow she gasped a few words into it.

'Take it slowly. Try again.'

PC Jones still sounded cool, in command of himself and the situation.

In a state of near panic Jenny tried again. There was a garbled acknowledgement that she did not understand but the driver seemed satisfied.

'How's he doing, Reg?' he asked.

'Bleeding's stopped. Breathing shallow, but that's better than nothing. His lips are blue and so are his ear lobes, so I'd say he's in shock. I only know a little first aid,' he apologised.

To Jenny he added, 'See if you can find his pulse.'

Grateful for something to do Jenny tried to find Peter Cole's pulse. It was weak and fluttering. She was dimly aware that she had been given the task to keep her occupied, and found that she did not mind. The police car raced ahead, blue lights flashing and siren blaring. Another motorcyclist thundered past, drawing alongside briefly before pulling away.

The conversation in the car sounded unreal to Jenny as PC Jones and Reg Collins talked, masking their feelings about what was taking place.

'What do you do, Reg?'

'Sales Rep. Used to be, anyway. I think my boss just fired me back there.'

'Is he your boss? Bit young.'

'Family connections,' Collins replied wryly. 'He's disqualified from driving, Mummy bought him a new two seater and I won second prize in the office sweepstake for guessing how long it would be before he lost his licence. Took less time than I thought but I got a tenner out of it.'

'I thought I'd seen him before.'

'Oh? I owe you a drink.'

'I'm off duty at ten.'

Jenny was reminded of the way some pilots had talked during her days with the airline when superficial chat masked intense concentration. She noticed that Reg Collins did not look away from what he was doing while he talked and his knuckles were white from the pressure he was applying to Peter Cole's injuries.

Another motorcyclist took up station behind them.

PC Jones remarked casually, 'Rearguard. He'll stay with us through the town in case some idiot does something silly.'

Their escort cleared the way with sirens howling like banshees, racing flat out to get Peter Cole to hospital, and Jenny knew the race might still be lost. She tried to make her mind blank, not to think that they might be too late, not to think about Harry, alone on the moors with only the cat for company.

***

Sergeant Harry Stoke stood at the edge of the small clearing holding two useless weapons, his own shotgun and Peter Cole's dart firing gun. Grimalkin stared at him from a spot about sixty yards away in the brownish heather. Stoke stared right back.

Experimentally, he swung his gun by the barrel, then did the same with Cole's. That felt better. He dropped the shotgun. Cole's gun made the best club.

'Right you bastard, I've had just about enough of you,' he snarled.

Harry Stoke strode off to do battle.

***

The insane dash through the crowded streets was a kaleidoscope of colour and the non-stop shriek of police sirens blaring as they flashed past Saturday shoppers, through red traffic lights, other motorists scattering like minnows fleeing from a pike. Every junction had a constable or traffic warden to wave them through and hold up other traffic.

Out of the frenzy of noise and motion Jenny heard Reg Collins say, 'We're losing him. How long before we get there?'

PC Jones eyes flicked across the mirror as he said, 'Couple of minutes.'

For the first time there was a hint of emotion in his voice. The tyres squealed as he pushed the car through a tight bend at a junction. Jenny found her bearings at last and knew there was only a short way to go. She could no longer feel a pulse. Peter Cole might be unconscious or, for all she knew, dead.

The wail of sirens cut off abruptly as the car charged into the hospital grounds. The doors were flung open and Jenny was shoved to one side as the emergency staff took over. A nurse pulled her away without ceremony and told her to stand clear to let a stretcher through. She allowed herself to be led away, feeling queasy all of a sudden. Her legs felt wobbly and her mouth filled with saliva. Recognising the symptoms she groped desperately for the blue bag she always carried in her flying overall, and she had to turn away while the nurse held her heaving shoulders until she was done.

The next hour was one of confusion, tension, and near panic, all rolled into one. Jenny managed to borrow a comb and do something to her hair, and splashing cold water on her face helped her calm down. Most welcome of all was a trainee nurse who mixed a mouthwash for her.

Superintendent Holley arrived with the welcome news that Sergeant Stoke had been found by the helicopter and was airborne on his way to the airfield where a patrol car would collect him and ferry him to the hospital. No, he wasn't injured, the superintendent merely wanted to see him.

Salesman Reg Collins admitted that his job was in jeopardy.

'The obnoxious brat will have a word with uncle. The chairman...' Collins shrugged his shoulders in a gesture that said more than words.

'Hmm, I see,' Superintendent Holley said. 'PC Jones tells me you're a good man to have around in an emergency, so if your company doesn't want you, remember there are other jobs. It's not all car chases and cops and robbers, in fact it can be bloody frustrating sometimes, but at the end of the day there aren't many better jobs. Think about it.'

After a brief handshake Collins left the hospital.

Arrangements were made to transport the microlight back to Jenny's hangar. It was never built to stand the rough treatment she had given it and Jenny had more than a suspicion that she had done major damage to the landing gear and engine mounts, and possibly to the whole structure. The Red Arrow might never fly again.

Superintendent Holley's uniform and Jenny's colourful outfit made them objects of interest but to Jenny's relief they were left alone. She did not think her overstretched nerves would stand much more.

Harry Stoke arrived by car and his bloodstained jacked was returned to him in a polythene bag. He made sure his shotgun ammunition was still in the pockets before he stowed it into the boot of the car that brought him. Then he went in search of Jenny.

There was nothing to do except wait. The hands on the wall clock seemed to stand still and there was no word about Peter Cole. Several times they put coins in the coffee machine and several times the cleaning staff removed their untouched cups.

Superintendent Holley attempted to get word from the operating theatre. A tactful staff nurse let him know that his authority stopped at the hospital door.

Well into the afternoon the same nurse gave them the information that Peter Cole was out of surgery. He was not fully conscious but with intensive care he was expected to make a good recovery. All three felt weak with relief.

'I'll get transport,' Holley declared, 'and I'm going for a stiff drink. So are the pair of you, we could all do with one.'

Jenny yelped, 'I can't go anywhere dressed like this!'

'I do my drinking in a nice little pub where I'm pretty well known,' Holley said, 'and my car and Sergeant Stoke's are on your field with civilian jackets to hide our clothes. We'll put them on and drive over to your house and give you just thirty seconds to put a coat on over your gear and tell them to put your dinner in the oven.'

Jenny gave in without argument.

In the Mobile Incident Room, manned at night by only two PC's on radio watch, Harry Stoke collected the gun that he had retrieved after the helicopter had picked him up. He stuffed extra cartridges in his pocket.

Superintendent Holley telephoned the hospital. There was no further news and he gave the number of the pub as his location and left instructions that he was to be contacted immediately if Mr Cole regained consciousness.

Using Stoke's car they drove Jenny to the farmhouse where she made herself presentable and threw a coat over her flying overall.

***

Peter Cole struggled back to consciousness. A dim figure sat in a chair by his bed.

Through waves of drug induced drowsiness he heard someone say, 'Lie still. How do you feel?'

Cole tried to lift his head. Moistening his dry lips with his tongue he asked where he was, feeling it was a silly thing to say.

'In hospital. You were attacked by the big cat. Try not to move, there's a drip in your arm and it'll sting if you move it. You were lucky, the cat could've killed you.'

The cat. Cole fought for awareness. There was something to do with the cat, something that he knew was important that he had to tell somebody. It was like a bad dream, he could not remember what he had to say, or who had to be told. Despite his efforts to stay awake he lapsed back into unconsciousness. The male nurse made a note on his record sheet.

When Cole woke again after an interval of about twenty minutes his head had cleared. He knew at once where he was and how he had come to be there. He had also managed to recall what it was that was so urgent. He knew what Grimalkin was going to do next, and he knew where and when. It was vital to inform Superintendent Holley.

The nurse listened closely to the words Cole gasped out, and then summoned assistance.

***

For a Saturday night it was a quiet place. From habit, both police officers sat with their backs to the wall, where they could survey the room. They took a corner table and Superintendent Holley was hailed by several customers who obviously knew him well enough to know when not to intrude.

Jenny was aghast when Harry Stoke described how she had flown off and left him without ammunition for his gun, and Grimalkin only yards away.

'It was my own stupid fault. Anyway, there was I, and there was Grimalkin, and my gun was empty so I picked up Peter Cole's where he dropped it, and when I found his was empty too, well, I wasn't very happy.'

Jenny knew that Harry was making light of his experience but she felt too upset to respond. It was her fault he had an empty gun. Harry grasped her hand.

'It was my fault,' he repeated firmly.

'I was lucky though. I was standing there looking a right idiot when the helicopter popped up and they asked me if I wanted a lift. Under the circumstances it would have been silly to refuse so I hopped aboard.'

His words were joking but the smile did not reach his eyes.

It was warm in the pub and Jenny was glad she had her back to the room so she could undo her coat without drawing too much attention to the way she was dressed. She was undoing buttons when the landlord beckoned and held his fist to his ear.

'Telephone. I'll get it.' Stoke said tensely.

He was back within seconds.

'Peter Cole is conscious. He's figured out what that bloody cat is up to, and it'll be at Brian Gleaves' place tonight!'

Chapter 17

Ronnie Gleaves was a hero and he ought to have got a medal or something for shooting the cat. Well, everyone knew it was dangerous, didn't they?

There ought to be a reward too and he should have been given a load of money. Well, for Christ's sake, if it hadn't been for his heroic action and quick thinking nobody wouldn't ever have known there was a killer cat. He should be given a really big reward for what he had done. The trouble was he wasn't appreciated. He could've been selling his story to the papers and all, couldn't he? They would've paid well and he would've told them how he held his fire until the last moment when the cat attacked him. Yeah, he would've told them just what happened. But modest like, because he was a hero.

They were all going to be sorry about beating him up and all that, and when he got his reward he was going to get a flash car. Then they'd be sorry.

Ronnie sat hunched in his van, slewed round in his seat with his knees drawn up to his chin, out of sight of the road and hidden from air observation. Ronnie's extensive knowledge of the moors and local country, gained through years of poaching, stood him in good stead and there was little chance of discovery.

The appearance of the van had changed. Ronnie had gone into a hardware store and emerged with a tin of blue paint and two brushes, and he had been forced to pay for the brushes because he was getting some funny looks. Well, they didn't know about the paint hidden in the lining of his coat and what they didn't know wasn't going to hurt them. He discovered the colour when he came to use it. It was blue.

He cleaned the side panels of the van, sniffing frequently while he worked, and using the smallest brush he wrote 'B.C.E. Window Cleaners. Tel 193-6309.'

With painstaking care he made a fairly neat job of the lettering, and with the paint left over he changed the colour of the roof, using the largest brush to spread the paint as he poured it out of the tin. That would trick them fools in their helicopter!

A plastic bucket hung from the grill and hid the number plate, and a stepladder poked of the back doors so that they had to be tied together. The ladder and a strategically placed rag obscured the rear number plate.

The bucket had belonged to the garage where he bought petrol, and the ladder had been in someone's garden.

Sniffer had driven past more than one patrol car without attracting attention, and when he had seen the helicopter and that yellow thing flying around they had taken no notice.

It was after midnight and just about time to get going but he needed money first. The should be some around the house and the old fool would be in Bristol so he could walk right in, and maybe he could find something to sell if he looked around a bit. Tools maybe, the stupid old bugger had plenty and he was always going on about how valuable tools were. Stupid old git! Sniffer calculated that he could spend an hour or two in the house and get something to eat and see what beer and stuff he could find and then get a bit of sleep before he left. Food would be the first thing, he was starved.

London was the place to be, he reckoned. He could soon make out in London and he'd have a flash motor in no time. Yeah!

He settled in the driving seat and turned on the ignition. The needle on the fuel gauge barely moved. Heck, he'd have to siphon some from the workshop to get anywhere.

The engine started noisily, he engaged second gear because first was a bit dodgy, and using dipped headlights he eased out onto the narrow road.

***

Sergeant Stoke drew extra strength from somewhere and he fairly crackled with energy, his voice crisp and his gestures economic as he drove at speed from the inn. Superintendent Holley sat next to him. Jenny was in the back.

'Peter Cole was only barely conscious but he did manage to get his message across. Putting two and two together, it seems that Grimalkin is making for Brian Gleaves' place.'

'Why there?' Jenny leaned forward to hear the answer.

'Well, as far as I can make out from what the hospital just told me and from what Peter Cole said when this started, Grimalkin is settling a score. Some cats are territorial remember, and Grimalkin is laying claim to its patch. Also, it's out for revenge. Sniffer shot Grimalkin and Grimalkin is out to get him.'

'There's no way the cat could know that Sniffer's taken off of course,' the superintendent interjected. 'I suppose it's returning to the scene of the crime, so to speak.'

'I don't think so sir. Rather, Peter Cole doesn't think so, he never was satisfied with Sniffer's version of events. Peter's theory is that Grimalkin knows its way around its patch and what it's doing is looking for Sniffer at the place where it's most likely to find him. At home, that is.'

Sergeant Stoke began to issue orders.

'Sir, I want you to use my radio to tell our blokes to keep out of the way, there's a freshly charged battery in my glove box with my radio. I don't want a load of coppers turning up mob handed with blue lights and sirens making enough noise to wake the dead.'

Glancing over his shoulder he said, 'Jenny, I'm dropping us off at Brian's yard. We'll stake the place out and you can drive my car straight back to the farm. No messing, I want you well out of the way.'

Jenny opened her mouth to protest, then thought better of it.

Superintendent Holley was an experienced man who had worked with Harry Stoke many times before and he knew he was not giving away any of his authority by allowing Stoke to give the orders.

He found the battery that Stoke had mentioned and slotted it into the radio. Something occurred to him.

'What are radio communications like from Gleaves' yard?' he demanded.

'Pretty good, usually.'

'Right. I want to be able to summon assistance if we need it. If you need it,' he added meaningfully, and Jenny suppressed a shudder.

She knew exactly what Holley meant. Grimalkin had already demonstrated a degree of resource and viciousness that she would never have believed possible. She desperately wanted to tell Harry to be careful, but she knew that would be unforgivable. She kept her fears to herself and prayed that nothing would happen.

The superintendent made his radio call, adding a request that his wife be informed that he would be late home.

'Very late, probably,' he added ruefully, and not into the radio, 'I rather think I shall be called to account for this to the tune of half a dozen new summer outfits.'

Stoke started to lay his plans.

'The house will be locked up and in darkness, with Brian away at his sister's place. That's good, because I really wouldn't want him to be there. The yard will be empty and... uh oh!'

Stoke broke off as he remembered something and he half turned to Jenny.

'Get Button out of it. Take her home with you.'

Jenny barely nodded. Stoke was not looking for conversation.

'Right then sir, the yard. The yard will be empty. It's pretty big and usually there's Brian's pick-up and Sniffer's van parked there, but not tonight. There's a woodpile on one side, with a sawing horse and a chopping block.'

Superintendent Holley recalled it from his recent visit.

'The woodpile will be the best place to hide up. Keep the radio handy but leave it turned off, I don't want anyone else's chat giving the game away. Now then, the barn is on the opposite side, and that's where Brian has his workshop. There wasn't a lot in there last time I was inside, just a bit of farm machinery and some bales of hay, or maybe straw, I wouldn't know the difference.'

Stoke paused to do some rapid thinking.

'The only light will be what moonlight there is, and as long as we don't get too much cloud it'll be enough. I've got a torch in the boot but we don't want bloody searchlights all over the place so I'm leaving it there. The big problem is whether we'll see Grimalkin when it turns up. If it comes in a straight line from where I last saw it this afternoon it'll walk straight in off the road, but I wouldn't count on it, that cat is smart. It'll be damned hard to see, but when we've got our night vision we should see quite a lot. And we'll be listening as well as watching.'

Superintendent Holley objected.

'I think we ought to have your torch. Perhaps we won't need it but I'd like to keep our options open,' he said.

'OK,' Stoke conceded. 'Maybe it's not a bad idea at that. If it comes to it you could shine the torch on the cat while I give it both barrels. I want to do the shooting,' he added, 'the Viking gun is made for this job, whereas your pistol isn't the best gun in the world for big game hunting.'

'Probably wouldn't even slow the beast down,' Holley agreed. 'I'll go along with you.'

Jenny Wells felt like screaming.

Stoke dipped the headlights and shifted into a lower gear as the car approached the yard. He slowed to a crawl and turned off the narrow road, halting in the middle of the yard. Nobody spoke as he turned the ignition key and the engine stopped.

After a long, long, silence the superintendent was the first to find his voice.

'Oh shit,' he groaned.

Button's kennel lay turned over behind the torn wire of her little dog pound.

Grimalkin had got there first.

***

Jenny sat alone in the car while Harry Stoke and Superintendent Holley cautiously reconnoitred the yard and barn while tears ran down her cheeks.

Stoke was not going to be caught without ammunition again, and he made sure that he and Holley had everything they needed before sending the weeping girl away. As the taillights of his car disappeared into the darkness the policemen were left standing in the middle of the yard.

'Over there Sir,' Stoke said decisively, indicating the woodpile, 'we'll hide up behind that. I'm more than bloody certain that damn cat is still around, and this time I'm going to settle a few scores myself. I want you to cover my back, and if you see or hear anything sing out and get the torch on it. And keep your head down so I can get a shot off!'

They moved into position. Holley stopped and pointed at the chopping block where Brian chopped his kindling wood.

'Sergeant, look there. The axe is gone. There was an axe laying on the chopping block when we arrived, wasn't there?'

'I didn't notice Sir.'

'You're probably right Sergeant. My nerves are getting the better of me.'

The superintendent disturbed an indignant chicken as they made for their hiding place behind the woodpile and he almost dropped his revolver as the bird fluttered away with an angry squawk. In the darkness he did not notice Stoke's gun swing round like a guided weapon seeking a target.

***

The woodpile was uncomfortable to lie on for any length of time and both men soon began to feel cramped and sought to ease their aching bodies with cautious movements. Stoke was certain the witch's cat was close by and would show itself sooner or later.

Superintendent Holley agreed, without being able to say why he felt that way.

As Stoke had predicted, their night vision improved, aided by the pale moon which shone weakly through wispy cloud. The night was calm and dry. And it was cold.

The superintendent found himself putting each hand alternatively inside his jacket and pressing it against his side to restore warmth to his fingers. His breath hung in the air like a ghost in the night and he wished he could light his pipe. The hot bowl with its little bonfire of tobacco would have warmed his fingers. Nothing moved.

Harry Stoke unbent his stiffened right knee and straightened his leg to ease the discomfort. He flexed his cold-numbed fingers around the trigger of his weapon, testing that he could still feel what he was doing. The metal parts of the gun were cold to touch. He laid his cheek along the wooden stock and brought the luminous dot on the foresight into line with the deep u-shaped rear sight, and aimed the weapon towards the poor broken kennel that had been Button's home.

Sergeant Harry Stoke hated the cat. With all his being he hated the cat, coldly, icily, with a rage that would not let go until Grimalkin was dead.

The long night wore on.

They kept their agonisingly uncomfortable vigil and the pale moon climbed into the night sky. The thin cloud drifted away, blown by a light wind, and the hard pinpoint lights of a thousand stars shone from a dark background of nothingness.

***

Ronnie Gleaves' constant sniffing was audible over the noise made by his labouring engine. The plastic bucked still hung over the front number plate but the ladder had been discarded, dumped by the roadside so that Ronnie could close the rear doors and keep in the warmth of the heater. In the deserted night he rattled along the road, swerving to avoid the holes along the verges where the metalled edges had crumbled.

One thing was sure, when he got it made in London he was going to have a radio in his car. And a player for compact discs and tapes. And a telephone too, yeah. A mobile phone would be all right. He could ring people up if he had a phone.

The fuel gauge registered empty and Ronnie tapped the glass with his bony knuckles without causing so much as a flicker.

It wasn't fair. The old man should have had more money in the house so he could have got more petrol and stuff. It wasn't his fault that petrol was so pricey and he had to pay out good money for fish and chips and stuff like that. And them games machines were crooked too. He kept on and on putting coins in the slot and he never even got his money back.

Bloody bastards, that's what they were, bloody bastards!

There was a bit of hose in the back of the van somewhere, so he could get petrol. Siphon one of the farm machines or use some of the stuff the old fool kept for washing down bearings and all that. Wouldn't be the first time. Ronnie sniffed loudly. The road was winding and narrow and the mistreated van complained at the smallest uphill climb so his progress was slow, but he would make it if the petrol lasted out. Groping on the floor he found a gritty piece of rag and wiped the windscreen, leaving smears of dirt.

His sigh of relief was audible even above the noise of the labouring engine and the rattles made by the junk in the back of the van when he saw the ungated entrance to the yard as he rounded the last corner and he knew he was going to make it. He made the right turn and ground to a shuddering stop near the workshop door.

Sergeant Stoke laid a cautionary hand on Superintendent Holley's sleeve when he saw the approaching dipped headlights. When the van turned into the deserted yard he uttered one word.

'Sniffer!' he whispered.

Automatically he checked the time of Ronnie's arrival, noticing with surprise that it was a good deal later than he had thought. With a start he realised that it had been getting lighter for some time and he could make out more detail than he could before. He shifted his weight just a little.

The superintendent risked a whispered word.

'Remember he's not what we came for.'

Stoke nodded, forgetting for a moment that the gesture would not be seen in the half-light.

'He's up to no good sir. The long streak of piss must know Brian's away tonight. We're going to have to pull him in.'

'Wait Sergeant. He hasn't given us reason to do anything yet.'

Both men were sure that before many minutes had passed Ronnie Gleaves would give them all the reasons they needed to place him under arrest.

***

The engine spluttered into silence with a dying cough. Ronnie Gleaves reached for his comb and slicked back his greasy hair before he got out of the vehicle. Switching off the headlights but leaving the sidelights on he opened the door and got out, shivering in the icy chill of the early morning air. He stuck his hands in his pockets for warmth. He was hidden from the view of the police officers until he stood in front of the vehicle, visible like a shadow in the faint light of early day and the dim light that shone through the uncleaned glass that covered the lights of his van.

Noticing the torn wire netting that had been Button's dog pound, and the overturned kennel that lay on its side he walked across the yard and stood in front of the wreckage. Stoke and Holley could almost have touched him. Stoke held his breath.

Gleaves aimed a mindless kick at the wire and turned on his heel and walked away.

Remembering his need for petrol he pulled the stuffed rag out of the filler neck and tossed it onto the roof of the van. Fumbling in his pocket he withdrew a box of matches that he rattled, then opened the driver's door and found a battered cigarette packet. He had just one cigarette left and he straightened it out and put it in his mouth. The flare of his match briefly illuminated his sallow features before he blew it out with his first lungful of smoke.

For the umpteenth time Superintendent Holley craved his pipe.

Ronnie tried the workshop door and tested the padlock that held it closed. Returning to the van he was lost to the view of the observing policemen until he emerged with a tyre lever that he used with some skill to wrench the lock off the door.

'The bastard's done that before,' Stoke muttered beneath his breath and received a grunt of agreement from Superintendent Holley.

The padlock was thrown to the ground and Ronnie pulled the door wide open. The red tip of the cigarette glowed brighter as he took in a long drag of smoke, standing in the doorway with the dark interior behind him. He turned his back on the yard.

When it happened both police officers were taken by surprise. A warning cough came from deep in the throat of the dark fury that seemed to shoot straight out of the ground in front of them, followed by an animal noise that made their hair stand on end.

The awful scream died away and Ronnie Gleaves, his pale sharp features twisted into a mask of terror, turned and raised his hands uselessly to ward off the thing that sprang at his throat. Before the shock-paralysed sergeant could act, Ronnie stumbled backwards through the doorway, brought down by the snarling creature that ripped his flesh, his agonised shrieks loud in the dawn of the new day.

His cigarette fell from his mouth and dropped a cascade of sparks as it fell and bounced off the doorframe. There was a flicker and a tongue of flame.

At last Stoke managed to bring his sights to bear on the dark thing that stood over the writhing body and he was squeezing the trigger when Superintendent Holley knocked his arm up.

'Don't shoot! For God's sake, don't shoot!'

Stoke triggered both barrels with a reflex action and twin spears of flame stabbed from his gun.

Holley was screaming, 'It's Windsley! Don't do it!'

Stoke felt as if he were moving in slow motion. He added his own cries to Superintendent Holley's.

'No Windy, no! Dave, don't go in there! Come back!'

The madly dashing figure of PC David Windsley came between Stoke and the cat as Ronnie Gleaves was dragged through the door of the workshop and tongues of fuel fed flame rose higher.

'Look out, he's started a fire!'

'It's all that waste fuel he dumped in the drain. The bloody fool's set fire to it!'

Against the glare of the flames the policemen saw the evilly snarling cat spring into the inferno, intent on the prey that was blindly crawling towards the flames. Without hesitation David Windsley followed and disappeared into the spreading sea of fire. Sergeant Stoke scrambled from his hiding place like a madman and raced towards the blazing building.

Whoomph!

A dull roar shook the ground and a rolling fireball engulfed him in searing flame. One of the drums of full of the fuel that Brian Gleaves had laboriously pumped out of the sump where Ronnie had dumped it burst as it ignited.

Superintendent Holley crouched low and threw his arm across his face to shield himself and dragged Stoke to safety, beating out the sparks that fell on their clothes and hair. Struggling with his burden he tripped, bringing the heavy weight of Stoke down on top of himself and knocking all the breath out of his lungs.

Inside the burning building the sound of screaming was suddenly silenced and another sound, the demented howling of a madman, died away.

Stoke regained his breath first.

'Thanks,' he gasped, coughing smoke, 'I thought I was a goner.'

Between Stoke and Holley there was no need to say anything else.

The furnace heat of the blazing building drove them back, knowing there was nothing they could do any more to help David Windsley or Sniffer. Or Grimalkin.

'The cat got the whole family in the end,' the superintendent said dully, and shivered at the thing Rita Windsley had become.

'She's pregnant,' he continued. 'The hospital told me. I expect you knew already?'

'Jenny told me, she was the first to know. They were so pleased about it, Rita and David. They wanted a girl.'

'I didn't know that.'

With a loud crash and a shower of sparks the roof of Brian Gleaves' workshop fell in.

Superintendent Holley's radio caught in the lining of the civilian jacket he still wore over his uniform shirt.

'If this thing still works I'll call in and have the fire brigade turned out. There won't be anything for them to do except go through the motions.'

Without wasting words he ordered the fire service to be called to salvage what they could from the wrecked building.

'And,' he said harshly, 'send the Coroner's Officer as well.'

The near empty fuel tank of Sniffer's van exploded in the heat and the van started to burn.

They stood in silence until there was a squeal of tyres and Sergeant Stoke's car with Jenny at the wheel made a sliding turn into the yard and skidded to a stop.

'I couldn't just go home and leave you so I drove a mile back up the road and parked the car,' Jenny said defiantly, 'but I fell asleep until just a minute ago and when I woke up it was getting light and there was all that smoke and, well, here I am.'

'I suppose it wouldn't do me any good to tell you to go home?'

The set of Jenny's jaw gave Harry Stoke his answer as Jenny flung herself into his arms.

The strident wail of sirens could be heard in the distance.

Chapter 18

The last length of fire hose was being coiled and stowed by a team of ash-grimed fire fighters while one of the big fire tenders was reversed out of the yard.

Several vehicles blocked the narrow road and two uniformed constables turned away the sightseers and kept the press out of the way.

Superintendent Holley was engaged in urgent conversation with a leading fire fighter when Jenny let out a stifled gasp and pointed towards the road.

'Button!' she exclaimed. 'It's Button! She's come back!'

The dog pushed past the crowd of people that were being restrained by the police officers and frisked her way into the yard.

Jenny went down on one knee to receive her and Button bounded into her waiting arms. There was a commotion on the road and she stood up to see Brian Gleaves push through the crowd, ignoring the cameras and the questions of the media.

Brian walked stolidly into his yard, standing aside for the reversing tender, and picked up Button as she left Jenny and rushed to him. Joining the superintendent and the leading fireman, Brian spoke first.

'Had to leave me motor back along the road aways. Sort of coming home early I was, because of leaving me dog alone and blow me if she wasn't coming up the road to meet me, and then I guessed something was up like. One of the firemen told me but I sort of knew already.'

He stopped, short of breath.

Nobody said anything until he spoke again.

Indicating the burned out van with a jab of his thumb Brian said, 'Ronnie was in the barn when it went up, wasn't he?'

Superintendent Holley laid his arm across Brian's shoulder.

'Sorry mate,' he said simply.

Brian stood still for some moments before he spoke in a quiet voice to his dog.

'We'd better see if we can find your bone,' he said, walking slowly towards the wreck of Button's kennel.

'Jenny, stay here with Brian,' Superintendent Holley ordered crisply. 'Sergeant, you come with me.'

The leading fire fighter stood aside to let them pass as Holley led the way into the ruined shell of the burned out workshop. Only the lower part of the outer walls was left standing, the timbers having been burned to ashes in the blaze. It was a scene of total destruction, with burned out machinery and charred beams still smouldering. Coarse black ash, water sodden from the fire hoses, clung to their shoes and clothing as they advanced.

'There.'

Superintendent Holley stopped and pointed.

Half buried under a fallen beam lay the charred remains of Grimalkin, the witch's cat. The wooden beam lay across the animal's outstretched right foreleg, crushing it.

'The Beast of Exmoor. It doesn't look so big now. I suppose we'll never know what it really was.'

'Nor where it came from. I'd have liked a better look at that paw before the roof fell in. Just to be sure.'

'That it was the right cat?'

A slight shrug of the shoulders.

'It must be. Mustn't it?'

They stared at each other.

A piece of machinery barred the way. Once it had been painted, now it was just a lump of heat-distorted metal. Kicking up more wet ash the policemen walked round it, and stopped suddenly.

The burned bodies of David Windsley and Ronnie Gleaves lay side by side. David's arm was outflung and the charred claw of his hand still grasped the handle of a small axe. The head of the axe was buried in Ronnie Gleaves' rib cage. The body lay on its back, the appalling features exposed to the sky.

Sergeant Stoke felt his stomach churn. He forced himself to ask a question.

'You knew, didn't you sir?'

'I guessed. I was sure the axe was stuck in the chopping block when we got here,' Superintendent Holley admitted.

There was a long period of quiet while they contemplated the bodies of the murderer and his victim.

Holley made a decision.

'Sergeant, we're none of us going to come out of this smelling of roses. I wouldn't want Brian Gleaves to know about this, he's taken enough stick already and it won't do anyone any good. I don't want Windsley's name dragged through the dirt either. Sergeant, I never thought the day would come when I would stand in court and tell a deliberate lie, but my evidence to the coroner won't mention this. I'll say that Windsley lost his life trying to save Ronnie from the cat, and that way there'll be a little money from the police fund to give their baby a start in life. God knows, it'll need it. I can keep you out of the court and see to it that you don't have to give evidence.'

He bent down and steeled himself to the unpleasant task of freeing the remains of the axe from the dead police officer's fingers, ignoring the sights and smells of what he was doing. When he came to pull the axe head from Ronnie's bare ribs he found Harry Stoke's firm hands helping him perform his ghoulish task. At last the axe was free.

Flinging it into a corner where it buried itself in ash, Holley remarked, 'I'm guilty of three offences. Perjury, destroying evidence, and concealing a crime, and the funny thing is, I don't feel guilty at all. Do you understand that, Sergeant?'

Stoke stood up straight.

'I'll be saying exactly the same thing sir,' he declared, 'for Brian Gleaves' sake as well as all the Windsley family. Let the muckrakers look somewhere else for their story.'

They walked out of the ruins without looking back.

Half way across the yard they were met by Brian and Jenny, with Button carrying her chewing strip in her mouth.

Shyly and with hesitation Brian Gleaves said, 'Something I got to say.'

He cleared his throat and looked up at the three faces, Jenny's, Stoke's, and Superintendent Holley's.

Diffidently he began, 'I want to sort of clear my slate and start fresh like, and I was talking to my sister in Bristol last night and she said I ought to as well. It's like this,' he lowered his eyes and shuffled his feet.

His listeners wondered what he was trying to tell them.

With an obvious effort Brian continued, 'Ronnie wasn't mine, nor never was. I had a cuckoo in my nest, but I never let on I knew, nor he didn't know it neither. See, nobody never did right by him, not really, so I sort of did what I could. I did my best, I really did, but he took after his mother too much. Anyway I wanted my friends to know, never mind them reporters from the papers nor anyone else what don't matter. Just as long as my friends know.'

Jenny's eyes blurred with tears as she bent down impulsively and planted a kiss on Brian's cheek, which made him turn crimson.

'I'm glad to be one of your friends, Brian,' she told him.

'That goes for all of us,' Harry Stoke added gruffly.

Superintendent Holley unloaded his revolver and put away the empty gun. Stoke's gun was still laying where he had flung it, ages ago it seemed to him.

Brian Gleaves had more to say.

'I been over the hospital once or twice to see her, Mr Windsley's misses I mean. And I took some flowers and they let me give them to her. I know about the baby, I sort of heard something what I wasn't supposed to. I know she ain't never going to get better neither, not really. I sort of wish I could do something.'

The information that Brian had been to see the living vegetable that had been Rita Windsley was not news to Superintendent Holley, who had his own ways of finding out, and he appreciated what Brian was trying to do, and at what cost to himself.

'I sort of asked if I could take Button next time I go because I read as how dogs help people get better sometimes. Gives them something to think about like. They said they'd see.'

'Anything that might help her has my full support and I know I speak for the whole force when I say that. I suppose the baby will have to be adopted. I'd like to see that it, uh, she, gets the best of everything.'

Wrapping his arm round Jenny's waist and holding her tightly, Harry Stoke replied, 'You needn't worry about that sir.'

Jenny blinked.

'Harry Stoke, if that's a proposal, I accept!'

She threw her arms round his neck.

When she released him at last she planted a kiss on the delighted superintendent's cheek as well, and gave Brian a second kiss on his.

Poor shy Brian could hardly contain his emotions and with his head in a whirl he found himself shaking hands with the men, being kissed again by Jenny, and promising Harry Stoke that he would sit on his side of the church at the wedding ceremony. Hardly knowing where to look he sought refuge with Button and picked her up. Dropping her chewing strip she started to lick Brian's face with her long wet tongue.

Making a halfhearted protest, Brian said, 'Blimey mate, leave off. All that kissing and all that licking, me poor old face won't stand it!'

Taking charge, Jenny told the three men, 'I think it's time I went home and told mother where her daughter has been all night, and I'll ask her to give us all some breakfast. And something for Button too, come on everybody!'

'No good arguing Brian,' the superintendent said.

To Harry Stoke and Jenny he said, 'You two get your car turned round while I get our man at the gate to drive Brian's pick-up back to the yard. Pick us up on the road outside, OK?'

Together the big policeman and the little engineer walked out of the yard.

Looking Harry Stoke in the eye Jenny said, 'She'll need brothers and sisters Harry.'

Their embrace was a long one.

Brian stopped and regarded the burned out ruin.

'I'm insured mate, so no damage done. I'm sorry about Ronnie but it was his own fault and I'm done with him. I sort of made up my mind a long time back. I got plans for a new workshop, what with the insurance money and a little bit I got put away. I've been having a word about them little engines like in Jenny's aeroplane and I reckon I can do them all right, and all the rest of it.'

There was an air of new hope about Brian Gleaves and Superintendent Holley was glad he had put the past behind him.

'I'm expanding mate, that's what I'm doing. In about three, maybe four months, I'll be doing all my old business and more besides. I'll have to take someone on though, I can't do the lot myself.'

'Someone to help with the work?'

'Everything mate. The lot. I reckon a part timer is what I want, someone what can do a bit of driving and some heavy work now and again.'

Wistfully he added, 'I could do with some help with the paperwork too, I never could be done with that.'

'What you want is someone with a clean driving licence who isn't afraid of hard work and can write letters and answer the phone and run your office. Someone who doesn't need telling what to do.'

'Reckon I do mate,' Brian agreed.

'In about three or four months time, I think you said?'

''S'right.'

'Uh huh. Brian, would you consider taking on a retired superintendent of police?'

'Cor, mate!'

THE END

The British Big Cat Society

The Aims

The BBCS has been formed to scientifically identify, quantify, protect and catalogue the Big Cats that freely roam the British countryside.

The Means

The British Big Cat Society is a network of people whose aim is to research, study and scientifically analyse the presence of Big Cats throughout Britain. This unique organisation enables data to be collected and distributed to and from its members.

The BBCS enables the public to report their sightings and Big Cat incidents to the society - who in turn will be able to assist the relevant authorities such as the Police, DEFRA and Wildlife organisations etc. in dealing with Big Cat sightings, evidence and situations as they arise throughout the UK.

The society will also be active in pursuing further conclusive evidence and is raising funds to undertake certain projects such as 'Trigger Cameras' and 'Hair Traps' in order to hopefully identify the species present, the numbers of animals, where they are located and any possible risk to livestock and humans.

The BBCS also wishes to see the British big cat population regarded as a (collective) protected species and safeguarded from the gun, as far as is reasonably practicable.

Printed in the United Kingdom
by Lightning Source UK Ltd.
9474800001BA